Carol Gibson

The End of August

By
Joyce Thompson

Published October 2000 by
Robin Thompson Charm School
17298 Lake Knolls Road
Pekin, Illinois 61554
309.925.3157
www.etiquette-network.com

First Edition

The End of August
Copyright © 2000 by Joyce Thompson

ISBN 0-9675318-1-0

Library of Congress Number: 00-192343

Cover design by Richard IV, New York

Printed in the United States of America

Dedicated to the memory of my parents, grandparents, and all my ancestors who diligently labored to enrich the lives of their descendants.

My heartfelt thanks and love go to:

My daughter Robin, who told me from the very beginning I could and should write this story, encouraged me along the way, and guided me through the publishing process. I could never have done it without you.

My husband Bob, who read and reread my story and gave me so many helpful suggestions. Thank you for the many times you told me how pleased Mom and Dad would be.

To my son Scott, for the computer graphics.

To Bethany, my granddaughter, for listening to me read these chapters to her over the years.

To my Aunt Frieda, who over the years has shared so much family history.
If not for her amazing memory, this book would be much smaller.

**My grandmother Anna
on her Confirmation Day**

The End of August

1

The fresh wood shavings on the floor gave a cozy yet heady sensation to the tiny brooder house. Dozens of baby chicks, peeping and scratching, created a sea of yellow around Anna's feet. Spring was her favorite time of year, a time to start over, the dreaded snow and ice behind them for another year. Winter was so confining. It was not as if she had anyplace special to go, but just to be out of doors, the anticipating of something, anything green pushing through the earth, excited her.

Sometimes she would brave the chill winds of early March to go to her garden's edge to discover the first tiny green spikes of the Star Of Bethlehem. Soon the creamy white, star-shaped blossoms would appear. The same light and carefree feeling washed over her each time it was revealed that winter was no more, never minding that soon she would feel summer's assault heavily on her back and brow. No! This was now and it was good. She bent to scoop a handful of peeping golden puffs and nuzzle the tiny chicks to her cheek. How could anything so soft and adorable grow into something so harsh and homely? "Shoo, go eat!" Anna commanded, and sent the little ones scurrying across their confines, their companions moving in a wave, and crowding the corners to escape the human sounds.

Outside it was warm. The rains had stopped and the dirt under the mulberry tree was finally drying. Anna stooped to remove the clinging shavings from her cotton stockings. She felt relieved to know that no one had seen her show affection for her chicks. It was not her way to be demonstrative, not her people's way. Times and life were hard and folks had to be hard to survive. Shielding her eyes with her arm, she squinted into the welcome sun. Its position told her that dinner time was close. She had just enough time to gather her girls from their play and prepare a decent meal.

Fred and the boys had been working all morning preparing the team and machinery for the long, laborious planting season. The clanging of the big dinner bell would bring a welcome break. All winter the farm lay deathly silent, save for the sounds of an occasional crowing or mooing, or the children's gleeful cries as they played in the snow. But now she heard birds, crickets, frogs, new babies in the barn, screen doors slamming; a whole symphony playing for her, bringing forth Spring!

The windmill gave off a lazy hum as Anna opened the gate leading into the yard. Another sound broke the tranquility, an urgent unwelcome sound. A horse and buggy raced into the barn yard, the driver bent forward as if to arrive faster. She immediately recognized Andrew, their neighbor to the east. Why a visit now? Should he not be as busy as her men this time of the day and season? No, only trouble could bring a body about. Andrew came forth and removed his straw hat. Tiny trickles of sweat ran from his balding head.

"Anna, you must come. Johanna has delivered her baby, but it lived only a few minutes." Anna's heart sank. Johanna was Andrew's daughter. She and her young husband lived on the farm bordering her parent's home place. Questions whirled through Anna's mind, but would have to be answered later. She knew without asking why she was needed. She would dress the baby. "No!" she wanted to cry out. "Not today. I feel happy and warm and good. I don't want this day to turn into what I know it will be." But with a firm command she sent the two oldest girls, who had come scampering at the sound of company, to go after Fred and the boys. Without stopping to wash up at the pump, her husband and sons approached, sensing something was wrong. Anna explained to them in hushed tones the tragedy that had brought Andrew. Fred took Andrew's hand and mumbled something, and Andrew shook his head, never taking his eyes from the ground.

Inside, her daughters were instructed to spread the table with fresh bread, apple butter, milk, and hot coffee from the cook stove for their Papa. The girls, too young to really cook a meal, were assured "We'll have a special supper."

Quickly washing her face and hands in the basin, and slipping on a fresh dress and bonnet, she headed for the waiting buggy and the dreaded task ahead. The bay trotted along at a slower pace, Andrew not pushing now. The two rode in silence, both wishing to prolong their destination. Anna twisted the buttons on her dress and gazed down toward the tracks the buggy wheels were grinding into the dirt. *How many times, how many babies?* It must be three, no four, little ones she had dressed. The first time was shortly after her own first born. Panic had swept through her as

3

she was led into the room where the infant lay. Alone, she raised trembling fingers to pick up the tiny garments to place on the child born too small to have even taken a breath. Sweat drenched her back and a sour taste rose from her stomach. She hardly looked—a transfixed gaze let her see only what she needed to. There. Done. I'll never do this again. But she had, and now again. Too quickly she felt the buggy swing to the left and start up the long lane. Mary, Andrew's wife, met her at the door. It seemed she had aged years since Anna had seen her at church last Sunday. Then there had been cheerful exchanges about Johanna's condition; advice and warnings. "The roads are clear, sign of the moon is good, Andrew is not in the fields yet, all should be well when her time comes."

Again she was led to a room to do what now seemed almost routine. She was struck with the perfection and size of the baby. Not small, not frail or infirm. As the gown was slipped onto the infant, the one the mother had so joyfully and diligently sewn in her months of waiting, Anna pondered, "Why did this little one not live? What was God's purpose and plan? Would there be discoveries made some day to save infants and youngsters from the dread maladies that struck countless homes?" She thought of tiny white stones that dotted the countryside marking the finality of lives that she thought should not have ended. She chided herself, "Thy will be done."

After tying the tiny bow on the bonnet, she said aloud, "There, you look just like you're ready to go Bye-Bye." The door quietly opened causing Anna to turn and see the ashen face of the father. With gentle hands she lifted the baby and placed it in the trembling outreached arms. She quickly left now, through the kitchen door, as the father made his way to the mother's room. And at that moment Anna felt another tiny layer of lead wrap around her heart.

Once again inside the buggy, it's gentle sway had lulled
Anna's drained body into a tranquil state. Her head
nodded, and she felt as if she could doze. The gentle
rocking continued. She was so tired. What would Andrew
think? She just wanted to sleep. Suddenly the buggy
stopped. She was jolted and grasped tightly to the buggy's
side. Wide awake now, her eyes darted wildly to grasp the
situation. It wasn't right. Her hands! They were the hands
of an old woman, and they were clasping the arms of a
rocking chair. How? She cried out in confusion and fear.

"Mom?" Emma entered the living room, smiling.
"Were you having a dream?"

"Oh, Oh yes. I must have been dreaming."

Things were familiar now. Her rocker, her living
room, the house in town. The late afternoon sun was
creeping into the west window, and again she found herself
waiting. Waiting for what? For Mrs. Maas to come and
care for her during the night?

"Come", said Emma, "let me help you to the kitchen.
I've made us some coffee. We'll talk about your dream. I'll
bet you were on the farm again."

"No," Anna surprised herself by declining. Nothing
pleased her more than to sit at her kitchen table and sip
coffee and munch rolls with her daughter. She knew Emma
would have to go soon to her own home and husband and,
although she lived close by, she always felt lost and
abandoned when Emma left. She comforted herself with
the fact that she would be back tomorrow.

"I think I'll just rest a little more, and maybe later we
can talk."

2

Closing her eyes to Emma's concerned face, Anna laid her head back and thought, *THE FARM, THE FARM....Why did I ever want to leave? Why? It was my life! And Fred, my God, it was hard on you. The day of the sale...your team, your machinery. Everything we worked for since our marriage. Through floods, illnesses, deaths, feast and famine, all handed over to another with the auctioneer's final cry. But I wanted a home in town. All those years of backbreaking toil, raising five children. I was getting tired.*

A city home had sounded new, fresh, sophisticated. Anna had imagined herself walking to market, chatting over a fence with neighbors, and shopping, but it wasn't like that at all! She was fearful. Even on their quiet street she felt intimidated by busy neighbors and fast traffic. Fred went daily to the farm they still owned but rented out. He puttered and helped the new tenant as he could, but Anna could not go back. Another woman was in her domain, so she and Elly, who never married, rose early as always and performed their routine tasks. The one and only consolation was her tiny garden that grew in the southeast corner of her back yard. Even that was a long time ago.

When did we come here? In 1940 something. My beloved Elly, my youngest, died in 1949. I can surely remember that. It would be some mother to forget her child's death. Yes, 1949. How old am I now? Fred's been gone a long time too. Four years after Elly.

Elly's death had ravaged Fred. Emma had found him crying in the back yard alone. Ashamed, he'd said, "I'll bet you think I'm a big baby." She had embraced her father's huge trembling frame and awkwardly tried to console him.

Anna had been alone a long time.

How old? Over ninety, I know. Almost one hundred. Who would have thought? She chuckled to herself. As a young woman the doctor had told Fred, "With her heart, she could go any time." *Well, I showed him!*

Sinking back into her slumber, Anna found herself busy in her kitchen. It was Christmas Eve, 1904. Her second wedding anniversary. Four years into a new century. Could it be possible? Her toddler son was underfoot waiting for the sweet warm surprise to be taken from the cook stove oven. This would be their Christmas treat. Kuchen and milk for their party. A twinkle in Fred's eyes said he was up to something. With a bed sheet folded under his arm he slipped out the back door into the icy night. Quite soon, a rap at the door startled the child. In swept Der Bensnikel. With the sheet covering his large frame, he approached the tyke to question his being a good or bad boy. Suddenly, the little one summoned all his courage, delivered a firm kick to the visitor's shin, and bellowed in German, "Get out of here, you son of a gun!" Anna and Fred, after the initial surprise, nearly collapsed in laughter. This tale was to be told many times in her long life.

Spring came and, with it, spring cleaning. While her son slept, Anna was on her hands and knees pushing the old worn scrub brush across the kitchen floor. The kitchen was the hub of the home in the winter, and it seemed the task of removing the remains of the previous season from the floor would take well into fall. Suddenly, a fearsome commotion brought Anna to her feet. "What in the world?"

Pulling open the door, she was astonished to see a ruffian with a bear on a leash. Never had she seen such a sight. A wash tub was at his feet. "For pennies...bear dance," the man proclaimed. What to do? It wasn't every day you saw a bear. In fact, Anna had *never* seen a bear, much less one that danced.

Where was Fred? Oh yes, he had gone to the river to fish. Throwing caution to the wind, she ran to the cupboard and fished two pennies from a small bowl. Keeping a safe distance, she tossed them into the air and the ruffian caught them in his tattered hat. At once he started beating the tub with a stick and the poor old bear stood on his hind legs and twirled in a circle. Anna was caught up in a child like frenzy and clapped her hands and laughed aloud. The grizzled old man, a toothless grin spreading across his face, the tired old bear, and a young farm woman-child, her long skirts whirling and bobbing, escaped for a few precious moments from their mundane lives.

Out of breath and dabbing sweat from her forehead, Anna sat on the porch step and watched as the unlikely pair plodded down the road.

Back on her knees, brush in hand, Anna pondered what a curious sight that must have been, her dancing with a bear on a golden spring morning in her front yard on this vast sand swept prairie. It was not until the following Sunday when neighbors related the story of the dancing bear, that Fred could believe a word of her excited ranting. He'd hoped she was just being her teasing self again. Since marriage and family she'd become subdued and mature. But oh, in their courting days she delighted him with tales and deeds that amused and sometimes startled him.

Both of their religious, stern parents would never condone any silliness or frivolity. But Anna was the baby of nine and the apple of her Poppa's eye, and surely many of her antics went unnoticed that would have proven quite unacceptable to her siblings.

For weeks neighbors chattered excitedly about how they had shunned the ruffian and his bear, told him to leave. Women home alone had peeked through windows at the awesome sight and breathlessly waited until the duo was seen plodding down the road at a safe distance. "Oh yes," proclaimed Anna, "we must never let someone like that on our property. God help us to think what could happen." And only Fred observed the slight flush and subtle smile that swept across her face.

Emma also noticed a smile cross her Mother's sleeping face and was happy to know she was having a sweet long ago dream.

3

The jars stood in rows like stately soldiers on the shelves of the summer kitchen. Her trophies proclaimed the final fruits of her labors throughout the steamy, long summer of 1914. They had been blessed with an abundance of fruits from the tiny orchard and the garden had done well. As Anna always said, "This will taste good when the snow flies."

Too soon though would come the long, laborious task of butchering. Yes, of course, neighbors came to help, but with the neighbors came cleaning, endless cooking, and prodding the boys to replenish the wood pile that seemed to be consumed by her cook stove so rapidly at this hectic time. She would need more wood for hot water for skinning, lard rendering, and then the part Anna detested most, the women's job of cleaning the intestines. She never stopped complaining about this. Of course complaining did no good, but it made her feel better, so she continued to complain. Then came the two days of frying down the sausage. The house, even upstairs, was filled with the delicious long awaited aroma of it. When the meat was placed across a slab of fresh bread and topped with her recently made catsup, the family was content and full for days. Sometimes the children would have sausage and molasses bread for a winter afternoon snack. Without fail, the girls would singsong their favorite little rhyme:

"I'm seepy, seepy, seepy,

and I yunsta go to bed,

but my hands are ticky, ticky, ticky,

from eating yassy bread."

Finally, when the hot liquid grease was poured over the sausage into the big stone crocks, a sweet sense of fulfillment washed over Anna. "But never mind, that won't be for a few months," she thought and she lifted her apron to wipe away the rivulets of sweat from her face.

Thunk! Anna was startled by the sharp intrusion.

"It's only the newspaper Mom. I'll get it," Emma offered.

"What's the headline?" Anna queried.

"Oh, something about President Ford flying someplace." Emma read the latest goings on aloud but Anna wasn't listening.

"Anyone we know die?"

"No, no one we know."

Anna's swollen knees ached. She hated taking her pills. They didn't help anyway. She'd eat something in a little while, yes, in a little while. Right now Anna had to bake a cake for her Poppa. She was eighteen again, and quite the accomplished cook.

The snow was almost waist deep when Poppa went to

the barn to check on the animals. In this type of weather, he
went to the barn at noon also to make sure there was plenty
of hay to tide them over till the night feeding. Anna knew
he also went because he had to get out of the house. Even
in blizzard conditions it was hard for a man to stay indoors.
He enjoyed the gentle sounds the cows made when he
unlatched the door to the stable, the steamy warmth their
bodies emitted. The great horses were silent, but their eyes
showed excitement and they flailed their heads from side to
side as if in greeting. He piled more straw around their
massive hooves. Poppa always marveled over the drafters
big feet.

Breaking a broom straw to test the cake for doneness,
Anna expressed concern to Momma. Poppa never stayed
out this long in bad weather. Should she go see to him?
Pulling on her long coat and wrapping a muffler around her
face Anna pushed open the door to ice and snow pelting her
squinted eyes. *I hate winter. Where is Poppa?* The path he
had trenched earlier that day was nearly half full already.
Now almost to the barn, she heard cries, whimpers,
agonizing, and then anger. In moments, she was at her
Poppa's side. His big navy blue coat loomed against the
heap of white snow he lie across.

"I tripped...the wagon tongue."

He was writhing now. Things whirled around her.

"Poppa!" she screamed.

"Pull me up!"

His face matched the color of the snow around him.

"No, lie still. I'll get Momma".

"Pull me up!" he commanded so fiercely that without a

second thought Anna pulled her father to a standing position. To her amazement she took his weight on hers and led him, hobbling on one leg into the warmth of the house. Momma's hysteria brought a take-charge calm to Anna. The nearest neighbor was only one mile away. She could saddle old Ned and get that far even in this weather. Mr. Knowles would then have to get the doctor for them. He would just have to.

"The leg is broken," the doctor proclaimed. "A bad break."

A handful of neighbors and kin had gathered by now. Anna wanted everyone to be away from there. She wanted Poppa to be sitting at the table enjoying her cake and pouring his hot coffee into his saucer to cool, bragging how his Anna made the best cake ever. But the cake had burned to a crisp and her Poppa lie in bed hurting, and the people were smothering her.

Anna crept up to her tiny room and lay on her bed. Her teeth chattered and she shook from both shock and the cold. Pulling the yellow and white quilt around her chin, Anna closed her eyes and let her mind race back to happier times. She was sitting at Poppa's feet listening again to the story of the big boat. He was on it for a long time. Yes, coming to a new land. Several people had died on the boat and even little babies. Anna listened with morbid fascination as Poppa told of the ugly sharks that followed them, waiting for remains that could no longer be held on ship. Even more dreadful to her was the thought of leaving behind his parents and brothers and sisters. His beautiful little village; leaving hearth and home when he was only eighteen years old. That had seemed old to Anna at one time. Now she marveled, *That's my age now! Eighteen. I could never go so far away!* Poppa had told of his mother's grief when she was told he was leaving. The day of his departure; telling his Momma and Poppa goodbye. Little Peter, only three years old. Adam, nine, trying to be brave. Two year old Maria had died just four years before, and still his Momma mourned. Jacob, Georg, Christina. Would he ever see them again? He'd visited the graves of Georg Peter, struck down at only nineteen, and Baby Elizabetha.

"I'll send for all of you to come to my new country. I'll be rich and have a home for you." And so he left. And they did come. Five years later. But Poppa's eyes would tell of the pain he still felt after all these years, because his Momma had not come. She had lived only one year after that gray, gloomy day when he had held her and heard her last words, "Don't go."

But he had come to his new land and had indeed prospered. Even so, her Poppa was now struck down. Anna helped care for him, talked to him, prayed for him, and for a time her Poppa seemed to rally, though the pain was constant. Then one day fever set in and a poison was sent through his body. Anna hardly ever left his bedside. The pain seemed to subside, but she knew Poppa was slipping away.

One evening her brothers and sisters had returned to their homes. Momma was in the kitchen washing the dishes from the light supper she and Anna had shared. Anna sat looking at Poppa. The ticking from the clock that had been a wedding gift to her parents seemed to fill the room. She idly gazed at the wedding ring design on the blue and white quilt that someone had labored on for so many months. For some reason she couldn't remember who had made it. The loud chime from the clock startled Anna. Eight, she counted. And just as the last chime had sounded, Poppa took a deep breath and let out a raspy sigh. Anna knew. Her Poppa had left her. A rain had started and was

14

gently tapping on the lace covered window. She pulled back the curtain and stared out into the cold darkness. The water running down seemed to blend with her quiet tears. Turning slowly, she stopped. Momma was standing in the doorway.

And so, in the first month of the last year of the nineteenth century, Anna watched through vacant eyes as her beloved Poppa was laid to rest.

4

Threshing season had ended. The anticipation, the preparation, the neighbors, the endless hours of baking and cooking ended too. Anna had thought she would surely melt from the heat given off by her stove that seemed to be burning night and day. She had cleaned cupboards, scrubbed everything in sight in her kitchen, and gotten out her best dishes and utensils. Wedding present linens were pressed; company things, these were called. Neighbor women would be invading Anna's kitchen. It could not be said that hers was not spotless. Finally the big day had arrived, a reunion of sorts. The men were all business, having arrived at daybreak. Anna could not remember her children scampering from their beds so quickly upon hearing the massive steam engine pulling the lumbering threshing machine into the farmyard.

In years past, Adam, who owned the rig; and Samuel, the water wagon man, had spent the night. Much to Anna's relief, this year she would not have the extra burden of someone occupying the guest room and more places to set at the breakfast table. Still, she would prepare a substantial breakfast for the family to sustain them through the long, strenuous morning till the noon meal. Her mind whirled back to months ago when Fred and his sons had planted the grain; observing them daily watch with pleasure as the field produced a lush green cover. Before she knew it, Fred was readying the grain binder, which would cut the golden carpeted field and tie the grain into bundles to be left on the ground. It was indeed a marvelous sight to behold when the bundles were stacked into shocks, dotting the countryside, sometimes as far as the eye could see. One especially moonlit night, she and Fred had stood at their upstairs bedroom window and looked out across the field at the ripened shocks. She loved this tranquil sight, and wanted to keep it in her mind forever.

Now the grain was ripe, and people were coming to clean the fields and leave behind only the huge straw stack which would delight her children for weeks. As soon as the sun hit the shocks Adam was ready to start. He was half way to completing his run of farms, hoping for good weather each day.

Soon the field was alive with teams of horses and hay racks. Men loaded the bundles of grain on to the racks with pitch forks. They pitched the bundles into the thresher which then cleaned and separated the grain from the straw. Fred watched with pride, yet concern, as the grain flowed into the wagons, yelling orders and directions as teams pulled the wagons to the granary. An unending supply of water was hauled to the steam engine, and it was every tiny boy's dream to be the driver of the water wagon. Philip, the separator man, had the responsible job of seeing to it that the thresher was properly adjusted, and that the grain was not blown into the stack with the straw.

And so it had gone all morning. The sun was getting hot and high in the sky, but no one noticed. The horses huffed and strained; the men toiled, laughed, repaired, shouted, and sweated. The machines labored, smoked, and displayed great power and intricate movement.

Inside the kitchen the women were toiling also. Fred had gone into the village the day before and purchased the biggest beef roast the butcher had. Even now the succulent meat was simmering in its rich juices. Never before had the girls peeled so many potatoes. That night, when they went to sleep, they would see potatoes before their eyes. Heads of cabbage had been thinly sliced for coleslaw; loaves of bread had been baked; pans of beans now baked in the oven; and the pies, lemon, apple, and peach, were cooling on the side board. Everyone was hurrying now to have the long table, laden with scrumptious victuals, ready for when they would hear the long whistle of the steam engine proclaiming the noon hour had arrived.

Outside, horses were fed and watered. Basins of water with plenty of soap and clean towels were set up for the sweaty, chaff covered workers to use before quietly parading into the house and surrounding the feast spread before them. Anna could not remember a year when someone hadn't knocked over his glass of water or milk. Apologies were begged and were accepted as she quietly wiped up and refilled the glass of the embarrassed offender. Cousins and neighbor children were at smaller tables in another room and had to be constantly refilled and rebuffed. The rarity of their visits with each other encouraged them to make the most of the day. Their playful antics and all the merriment surrounding them on this wonderful occasion would long be ingrained in their memories.

At the big dinner table, the men were slowing down. Even with the urging by Fred to "eat your fill," plates were being pushed aside. After profusely thanking Anna for her work and hospitality, the men lumbered to the front yard, and like so many head of cattle, slumped to the cool grass under the huge shade tree. Only Fred and Adam noticed the dark clouds that had arisen while they had been inside, an ominous sight for a threshing crew. "Let's go! I don't like the looks of it," someone shouted. Once again, with great precision and comradeship, the fields were alive with the frenzy of man, beast, and machine. Throughout the afternoon and into the evening they worked, striving to beat the rains that were sure to come. As the last worker and animal left the field, the last grain bin latched, and all was finished, the heavens opened up and Fred ran for the house. Anna, waiting at the door, proclaimed, "You're soaking wet. You'll surely get sick!"

5

The harvest was done, the barns were full. A complete sense of fulfillment surrounded the farm. The rains continued throughout the night and into the next day. The rest from outside activities was needed and appreciated. On the third morning, Anna awoke to the faint peach rays of sunlight framed around the window shade. Good. The rain had stopped. Had she overslept? It was so quiet. The old clock in the parlor chimed. Anna held her breath and counted. Six! Fred still sleeping? The animals needed tending. Wide awake now, she nudged Fred's shoulder. "Wake up! The cows will be bawling if you and the boys don't get out there and milk soon. I'll start breakfast."

"Could you bring me a drink of water?"

Anna spun around. He was flushed and made no effort to move.

"What? What is it?"

"My throat, so sore. Water please. I'm so hot and dry."

Within a moment Anna had run barefoot down the cold steps to the water bucket and was back at his side with the dipper. With great effort he sipped and swallowed and fell back to his pillow.

By then the bleary-eyed boys had appeared at the door. "Your Poppa is sick. Go to the barn. You know what to do. If you need help, come get me."

The girls were frightened and crying. Poppa sick? Poppa was never sick.

"Emma, get your sisters something to eat. Keep them out of the way. I'll send one of the boys after the doctor when milking is done."

"No, I'll be fine. Just a little time lying here, I'll be fine."

Anna lost count of the times she climbed the stairs that day. The family and farm needed her attention, but so did her sick husband, because he wasn't fine by afternoon. He was feverish and restless, still only taking small sips of water. She dreaded sun down. *What if he gets worse?* There was little she could do, so she wrapped herself in a warm quilt and sat all night in the rocker by his bedside. The kerosene lamp flickered a soft glow, and her eyes were drawn to it. Her lids became so heavy that she dozed, but was jerked awake by his every move. So the night, which seemed like three, passed.

Some time toward morning, Anna, still exhausted from threshing day, dreamed she was back in school. The tiny school room was vivid and it was her turn to recite, but she couldn't remember. The palms of her hands were cold and damp. Every one was staring at her. She knew her lesson so well, but she couldn't remember! Sobbing, she turned and ran outside into the school yard, but she fell with a great jolt and then her eyes flew open. Now she was stiff and sore from sitting up all night. Anna longed to stretch out under the warm blankets and sleep forever. Fred's eyes were open.

"How do you feel this morning?" He tried to speak but could make no sounds. His throat seemed swollen even on the outside.

"I must look in your mouth." Fred turned his face into the pillow as if to escape his misery. Raising the window shade for light, Anna forced the dry, cracked lips apart. She held the handle of a dinner knife on his tongue. "My Good Lord. We must get the doctor."

Anna was in the kitchen preparing for the doctor's arrival when she heard movement on the stairs. Fred, fully dressed, was making his way unsteadily to the table. "You're crazy! Get up to bed. Hurry on! The doctor will be here soon."

"I'll see him like this. Not in bed. Help me to the porch. I want the sun." Angry, yet amazed at his endurance, she helped him outside to sit on the wooden chair with the high back. His arms were limp and he was shivering. Returning to the house for a blanket, Anna stopped. The doctor! He's here.

The doctor made his way to the back door with the children tagging closely, their curiosity aroused by the mysterious secrets contained in his bag but keenly cautious of this man who held the power to both heal and hurt you. Little Elly suddenly had a surge of recollection. This was the same person who had pushed and prodded on her tummy and given her something bad tasting that Mama had to put sugar in before she would swallow it. With an outburst of tears, she clung to her mother's skirts. "In the house—all of you, till I come and get you! Not a sound!" When Mama used that tone the children knew not to argue.

"Fred, Fred...Now what's this all about? A nice day like this and you're not out fishing?" Fred responded with a weak, forced smile as he watched the doctor open his bag and bring forth fearsome looking instruments. He was ready to receive help, though. "Anything," he thought, "Just do it!"

The doctor wasn't quite prepared for what he saw, and Anna noticed a slight wince. Quinsy sore throat! One of the worst cases he'd encountered. "I want clean towels and hot water." While Anna hastily prepared for the doctor's needs, Fred was vaguely aware of the doctor's polite conversation commenting on the recent threshing and that of their nearby neighbors'—whose was finished, whose was delayed because of the rains.

Everything was ready. Anna started to hold Fred's hands. "No," the doctor shook his head. "Let him hold the arms of the chair. He'll hurt you. Now Fred, you'll have to keep your mouth open wide. This will help." He produced a cork and placed it snugly in the corner of his mouth. Fred wanted to escape. The cork gagged him and he couldn't swallow, but the pain and fever he was enduring had reduced him to helplessness. He closed his eyes to wait, but was suddenly invaded with intense, searing pain as the doctor gently drove the lancet into his abscessed throat. A sound arose from him that caused Anna to cover her ears. She was sick, too, sick at this sight. Fred's eyes were wide open now, hands clenching the chair so tightly that they were milky white. The doctor shook his head. "We must try again." Once more the lancet was thrust. And again. "My god, My god, help me! I can't stand it!" Fred silently prayed.

Anna had turned her back, burying her face in her apron. She wanted to lunge at the doctor, to push him away, to make him stop, to hurt him as he was hurting her husband. As for Fred, time stood still. There was no one in the world now but himself and the doctor. He concentrated on the doctor's glasses, a diversion. He tried watching the metal piece across his nose, and noticed the sweat running underneath. The pain had been so intense, he had started to feel a numbness overtake his body, almost a loss of consciousness. With yet another lance, Fred felt a tremendous release. Anna turned just in time to see the terrible thing that had caused her husband's misery leave his throat with a projectile force. With trembling hands, the doctor finished his work, cursing silently for the ordeal he had caused his patient to endure. *I did my best. There was no other way.* Done. He sat on the porch railing and felt himself go limp. *I suffered too. This gentle, kind man. Why did it go so poorly?* Sweat had soaked through the back of his shirt and now a breeze caused it to feel cold and clinging. "Let's get this man to bed." The trio weakly made their way into the house and up the stairs, while the little ones peered wide eyed and silent from the next room.

6

Emma noticed her mother's restlessness. She seemed miserable in her rocking chair. Gently she shook her shoulder.

"Here, drink your coffee. I have mine. We'll sit in here."

Anna had a hard time waking up. Yes, she needed her coffee.

"Remember the time your Poppa had such a bad throat? I've been dreaming about that. It was as real as when it happened."

"Yes, I'll never forget that. I remember being in the house when you and Poppa and the doctor were on the porch. I cried and cried because I knew my precious Poppa was getting hurt. The boys kept saying Poppa was going to die and I cried harder."

"He almost did," Anna remembered. " But you know your Poppa. He was up in a few days and then in a few weeks he was good as new. I can't believe how long ago that was."

"Would you like to go back to that time, Mom?" Anna pondered the question a long time.

"Would I like to go back? No, no. I don't think so. There were too many bad times. Oh yes, I'd love to see my family again. They're all gone but me. Emma, I tried to think. How old am I again?"

"Ninety five," reminded Emma. "Almost ninety six."

"Ninety six," Anna repeated and rested her head on the back of the chair. She had lived longer than anyone in her family that she could remember. "You know what I wish? I wish my Poppa could come back and see things now. He'd never believe it. The traffic and airplanes would scare him to death. I wonder if he'd ride in a plane. I never did, but I just bet maybe he'd do it." Thoughts of her Poppa riding finely in his surrey mingled with the thought of him riding in an airplane. The contrast! "But I'll just bet he'd do it" she smiled.

She was remembering but she didn't want to sleep. She wanted to talk and tell things as if to preserve them. "Momma was hard on us." Anna was speaking as if to herself. "If I didn't do something just right, she'd yank my hair. But sometimes I think back at what she had to put up with. Dirt floors were common then and that's what she had at first. Look what I have now compared to when I was young! Even then I never dreamed of such things. What would they think of my television and bath room? Emma, do you remember the night we got lost in the snow storm coming home from Momma's?"

"Do I! I've told my kids about it many times."

Sipping her coffee, Anna sat up a little straighter in her rocker. She wanted to tell it again. Emma listened. "Your sisters, you and I had gone to Momma's to take something. I don't remember what. When Fred hitched Old Babe to the buggy he warned not to stay too long. The air was right for a big snow, he said. But we hadn't been there for a while and time got away. When I looked out it was getting dark and snow had started to come down with a driving force like I'd never seen. By the time I got out on the road I couldn't see anything. Oh, how I wished I'd never come! You girls tried to help me see but it was of no use.

Remember how we tried to see the first farm house we had to pass? But the dim kerosene lamps weren't bright enough to light a window on this night. Old Babe was sure footed, but the snow was pelting her face so hard and she threw her head back and forth, I guess trying to see or escape the snow. It was so black out. People don't realize how black the nights used to be...Finally I admitted to myself I didn't know where we were or how long we'd been driving. I knew your Poppa was sick with worry. I covered you girls with the blanket and had you huddle at my feet. Then I just dropped the reins and said, 'Go home Babe, go home.' Poor old Babe trudged along. It seemed like forever. I prayed. I don't know how many times I said 'Go home Babe.' Then I felt the buggy turn. I was scared. I braced myself for a fall into the ditch. But she trotted now. We were moving fast. I held tight and closed my eyes. We stopped...I opened my eyes. No snow.

It was light. We were in the barn! Old Babe had brought us home right through the open barn doors with your Poppa standing there with his lantern. I don't remember ever being so happy to get home before or since. I don't guess you girls realized the danger we were in."

"I knew Mom. I was old enough to know. I thought Poppa would hug us to pieces. And Babe got treated pretty good after that," laughed Emma.

Old Babe, Anna thought. Whatever happened to you? Thank you for saving my family that night. Anna closed her eyes. Not sleeping. Just resting.

Emma looked at her Mother. Drank her in. *She's old now. How long will we have her?* She would miss her. The morning and night telephone calls, the ones in between. Emma went every day. She was not young herself anymore. She rubbed her eyes that were blue like her Poppa's. She was tired. She'd go home soon.

Her Mom's tan oxfords were laced around swollen ankles. Her knees were swollen and chronically aching. Her once plump body was thinner now, especially around her shoulders which seemed to droop into the shape of a clothes hanger holding up her navy dress with the tiny white and pink flowers on it. Her arms were covered with dark wine bruises that developed from the slightest bump. And yet, even though the skin hung loosely, Anna's arms still seemed strong and large. Her hands encircled her coffee cup and the opal ring that Fred had given her so many years ago graced her finger. Her hair was cut short and permed but was still not snowy white. Her face had the lines of someone who had known sorrow, hard work, laughter, and pain, and her eyes looked tired even when she wasn't. Still, it didn't seem to Emma that this was a person almost a century old. *Maybe it's because I don't want her to be old.* And Emma had a searing desire to be young again, and to have her Mother young. *How cruel time is! How it ravishes our bodies! Everyone wants to live to grow old, but why? But at least Mom's mind is good.*

Anna still surprised and amused her grandchildren with her quick wit and sharp memory. Emma sat and looked at her until Anna began to talk again.

"So many things happened when I look back. Now they all run together, but it took a long time for them to take place. What about the time you and your sister found the tramp in the barn? Was it summer? I know I sent you to hunt the eggs."

"Oh, I try to forget about that," Emma declared. "I still

get the shivers when I think about it. We ran to the barn with the egg basket and tried to see who could jump over the manger. Well, I was bigger so over I went. There he was, sitting in the straw. I can still see him. He was wearing some sort of uniform or something with stripes on the sleeves. I couldn't scream, I couldn't even breathe. The next thing I knew we were running as fast as we could to the house. I was pulling Sis and we fell. We both tore the knees out of our stockings."

"Yes," smiled Anna. "I had to throw them out. I couldn't mend them. When I saw you two I knew something was awful wrong. It took forever to get the story out of you."

"Well, we were too scared to talk! And Poppa and the boys were way out somewhere in the fields. I remember you locking the door and waiting for them to come home."

It was quiet. Anna spoke.

"I'd have gone out and rung the dinner bell. That would have brought them home. But I couldn't go out. I was afraid he was still around. How long did we wait? It must have been a couple of hours. When I saw your Dad and brothers coming across the field I got brave and ran out. I told them what happened, and your brothers got eager and started for the barn. One of them had a pitch fork or shovel or something. 'Not without your father,' I yelled. The closer they got to the barn, the more cautious they got. By then Fred had caught up. Well, as you know, they hunted all over and never did see him. He was long gone. I imagine you scared him just about as much as he scared you. To this day I wonder where he came from and where he was going. Maybe running away. He must have been tired and stopped in our barn to sleep. I wonder what ever happened to him. Wouldn't it be nice to know? But...we never will."

"But, remember Momma, we had another tramp a few

years later!"

"Oh yes, goodness, how could I forget that one? Your brother was pitching hay in the mow, and he jabbed him with the pitch fork. He'd been sleeping there all night. Well, he got an early waking up! But at least he saw the tramp leave. He had a bicycle, remember? He was so shaky and wobbly, and probably hurt, he could hardly ride. And it was weeks before your brother would go up in the haymow without a lantern. At least that one was seen going down the road. I wonder how bad he was hurt. No one else ever saw him. That's another one we'll never know who he was or where he was going or if he ever got there. Honestly, honestly! Life used to seem so dull sometimes. But when you look back, I guess I did have a lot of excitement in my life." And Anna seemed pleased that she did indeed have many things in her life that were not dull and forgettable.

7

Emma removed the cup from her sleeping Mother's hand. Yes, her Mother did have some exciting times in her life, but it seemed the excitement had been centered around hard work, danger, sorrow, and illness. When were the good times? Where was the fun in the their lives? Emma thought back to her own childhood. There had always been hard work. Up early, go to bed early. There was a chore each day. Washing on Monday. Ironing on Tuesday. Baking on Wednesday, and so on. Oh yes, and sewing the clothes. Even now, Emma didn't like to sew. She had spent so much time helping Poppa and the boys with their chores that she didn't get to learn the arts of sewing, knitting, and crocheting that so many women her age had mastered.

It was a peaceful existence. Everyone lived the same way. No one had much more or less than anyone else. Of course, the highlight of the week was church on Sunday. There you saw neighbors and relatives gathered together. The country church yard was overflowing with horses and buggies. After the service, once outside, the ladies clung together in tight little groups, thirsting for news and happenings over the past week. The men also took this opportunity to bring each other up to date on important issues, but the conversation invariably turned to crops, livestock, and farming in general. Mostly, though, Emma remembered the children. Dressed in their Sunday finery, elated to see friends and cousins, they gleefully ran and chased and darted in and out among the adults. Mothers admonished not to soil or damage a dress or pant, or scuff a shoe. Little boys pulled on little girl's braids. Little girls yanked off little boy's hats and ran with them. Older girls stood on one side of the yard giggling and whispering. Older boys stood on the other side and shyly watched the older girls giggle and whisper. Then all too soon, the parents had to round up the family so Mother could serve the big Sunday dinner that she had started early that morning. Anna had always served fried chicken or roast beef; and, occasionally, they would have guests for Sunday dinner.

Those were wonderful times. Company. Someone to play with besides brothers and sisters. Another adult for Momma and Poppa to talk with. Momma would set the table for breakfast the night before, as she did every night. On Sunday morning there was a hurried breakfast and dishes to wash, then the good dishes were brought out and carefully placed on the Sunday tablecloth. The bread and pies had been baked the day before, meat was put into the oven to simmer, and all but the finishing touches would be ready when the family, followed by their guests, would drive their buggies into the barn yard. Emma remembered one particular time when the children had gotten a case of the giggles during prayer time. It couldn't be helped. It was contagious! The stern reprehension they had received as soon as the guests were out the door, however, stayed in their minds; and it was, to be sure, the first and last time a case of giggles would occur during prayer time.

8

Anna heard a hammering sound. Unpleasant! Her mind tried to push it away. What was it? It became louder. Someone was on their farm house front porch. She recognized Supervisor Hofriter. Now it came into focus. With a sense of dread, she read the sign: QUARANTINE. She felt drained. Not again! This couldn't be happening again. But it was. Little Elly had again contracted Scarlet Fever. The memory of the previous quarantine was still fresh in her mind. For six long weeks Anna and the children were virtual prisoners in their home. She had fixed Fred his own room so he could live away from his family. He would be their only contact with the outside world. This way, he could ride into town for food and supplies and would do the chores and tend to the needs of the farm. Fortunately it was the dead of winter, so one person could handle the work load.

For Anna it had been a long nightmarish situation she prayed never to have to face again. The fact that her child was so ill was enough, but she had four other healthy children closed up inside wanting to play outside in the snow, wanting to go to school, wanting to see their Poppa. By the end of the first week Anna felt totally oppressed.

She kept a watchful eye on the children for signs of

33

illness. *We could by trapped like this for months. If the others or I get sick it could go on and on.* It had happened in other families she knew. Anna had lined up the children and given them food from the same spoon Elly had eaten from. Now they were all exposed. If they were to be sick, it would be soon and be over with.

Anna was up most of the night keeping a watchful eye on a feverish child. It was almost routine now, interrupted sleep, so better to continue the pattern. She remembered the ones who didn't survive the many maladies that took their toll, though, so her true concern was for her baby to get well.

By the end of the second week, Elly was getting better and so far everyone else felt fine. The days went slowly by. The children, impressed by the doctor who had visited, enjoyed playing doctor and nurse, and had their own imaginary sick room. Also, bridges, towers, castles, and barns with fences, were created with dominoes. Finally, the six weeks had passed and everyone was well.

Time to fumigate. It took a long time to prepare the house. Books had to be opened and stood on end. Everything had to be exposed so that the fumes could penetrate every nook and cranny, every corner and every surface, both upstairs and downstairs. Much to the children's delight, the day would be spent in the chicken house. The section that was divided for the baby chicks would serve as their home. The weather had warmed and the new found freedom brought whoops and hollers from the little ones, but no one felt more relief than Anna. Stepping outside for the first time in weeks, she felt a rush of fresh, moist air on her face. She breathed in deeply, and gulped the air. The winter enclosure, lack of sleep, exhaustion, and listlessness had left her skin and eyes dry. Her hair felt brittle, and she was wan and pale. She too, wanted so badly to run and whoop, embrace the out of doors, join in Ring Around the Rosy and fall down with her children. But no, back inside.

Anna had prepared a ham, potatoes, and baked beans to sustain them during their one day sojourn to the brooder half of the chicken house. Her children thought of it as a great adventure, sitting on boards to eat, having a 'new home'. Nothing could be brought outside except the food and bare essentials with which to eat. But no matter, the joy of all being together again, of having Poppa sitting with them at meal time, having Elly well, made this a special day. Anna reveled in it. She pushed away thoughts of the putrid odor that would greet her when she opened her kitchen door. The windows would have to be opened wide to permit fresh air to exchange with the old, and because it was still late winter, the stoves would be working relentlessly to reheat the house. Mirrors would be blackened from smoke and have to be cleaned tomorrow, but now five children were running to the barn to see the animals that were thought about so often. Small mittened hands quickly formed snowballs from patches hiding from the sun beside a building. Although the girls outnumbered the boys, as always, through shrieks of "I'll tell Momma," the boys claimed victory as their sisters ran to the brooder door to take cover and have Poppa brush the snow from their parkas and braids. After noses were wiped and the boys were scolded, once again the barn yard was full of the sounds of children, the sound that had been absent for so long.

And so the winter had passed and the quarantine was to be again. Where would little Elly have had contact with Scarlet Fever a second time? It must be a bad dream. It wouldn't happen twice! But no, the sign was posted. Her daughter was sick. With numb resignation Anna again began to prepare for the inevitable imprisonment that would divide her home, test her faith, and possibly cause her to lose a child.

It had seemed easier the second time. She knew what to do, and the children knew what to expect. But it was much harder to see her little daughter experience this disease again. Anna had the uneasy feeling that even if Elly fully recovered, she would somehow be weakened by this fever that had invaded her young body once more. That very same feeling would indeed wash over her years later as she and Fred would hear the doctor confirm his belief that having had this illness twice was the main factor in her contracting the disease that would eventually take her life at only thirty-six years.

At first Anna had thought Elly's sore throat had been caused by getting wet in the snow. She had taken her broom and swept the girls clean after they had frolicked in drifts and made snow angels. They had huddled around the stove and Anna had given them warm milk to warm their insides.

Two nights later, however, when Elly refused her supper, Anna placed the back of her hand on a hot forehead and peered at a very red throat. She'd held Elly on her lap while the family had eaten their meal; but the little girl was miserable, so Anna took her upstairs to bed. Fred had stayed with her while Anna and the two older girls washed dishes and cleaned the kitchen, but he soon summoned Anna to come. Elly was having a chill. They had brought blankets and wrapped her tightly, and Anna had held her while the child trembled and her teeth chattered. 'My baby,' Anna thought, 'What's wrong?' She pressed her cheek against the child's dark hair and felt the fever pouring out. Fred had gone to get her a cup of cold water while Anna pressed her lips on the part in the braided hair and murmured words of comfort. Her mouth burned as the fever ravished her little head. Sips of water failed to soothe the throat.

Finally the chills passed, and Elly wanted to lie on the

cool pillow. Fred brought a cloth and bowl of water for Anna to bathe the child's forehead. Instructing him to bed the older children, Anna continued to care for Elly. She refused their pleas to come and tell their sister goodnight. "I'll be in later, but you mustn't be near Elly now." With whimpers and questions, the youngsters padded down the cold hallway to snuggle in their feather beds and pray for their little sister. At Anna's insistence, Fred went to his own bed while she huddled under the blankets and softly hummed lullabies. She had heard the clock chime two when Elly suddenly became very restless and agitated. She sat upright and vomited. Anna threw open the door and called to Fred. "I need help!"

Fred spoke in soothing tones as he assured Elly it was all right and washed her tear stained face. As Anna slipped off Elly's soiled gown, she froze. There it was. The rash! Just as before. "Fred!" He turned ashen and reached for the lamp to have a closer look. It was there for sure. Red pin points spreading across her neck and chest. But it can't be. She's already been through this. Panic surged through Anna. She wanted to run from the room, to go outside. But now her baby was crying and telling her Poppa her head hurt so. Fred cradled her and felt her little heart pounding so hard and fast in her heaving chest, but they were totally helpless to give their child any relief. "I'll get the doctor at day break. It's snowing hard, but I'll bring him back." Numb with cold and worry, they spent the night bathing her feverish forehead, saying silent prayers, and listening to the icy snow blow against the window pane.

When at long last the bright sunlight shone into the room, Anna raised the shade slightly to look out. The window was frozen and a tiny drift of snow lie on the sill. Elly was sleeping, and Fred quietly rose from the chair and rubbed his neck. "I'll go make us some coffee. The roads will be bad. You must get started," Anna whispered.

The kitchen was cold. Anna's shoulders and neck ached from it and from lack of sleep. At least everything was in order from the night before, and the other children were still sleeping. The coffee was boiling when she went to open the back door, and she beheld a wondrous sight. During the night the storm had iced a glaze on everything. Every intricate detail on every object was glistening. The fence looked as though a snow fairy had taken her brush and outlined every wire with diamond dust. The trees were raising great crystal arms to a blue sky. The door knob on the pump house, the towering windmill, a bucket hanging on a post, even the fruit cellar doors, were now things of sparkling beauty. But the cold! It cut into Anna's lungs and caught her breath. She returned to the now warmed kitchen for a cup of water. Standing on the door sill before the icy porch, she threw the water high into the air and, before it reached the ground, it had turned into icy drops.

Fred stood behind her. "She's still asleep." He ate his breakfast in silence, pondering whether to take the buggy or to go on horseback. He would go directly to the doctor's home at this early hour. He would take the buggy, he decided, as the roads were surely treacherous. That way he could bring the doctor and return him to his home, rather than expect him to make the trip on his own.

Anna had awakened the boys to start the morning chores. It would take much longer this morning because of the ice, and, because Poppa wouldn't be there to help them. Doors, locks, and pump handles would be frozen. They would take the hot water she had in the kitchen to thaw the pump first. There were thirsty animals. She would need much hot water today. Anna had already carried a mound of clothes to be washed from the sick room out to the wash house, where she would heat the water in the copper boiler. Supplies were needed from town because of what lie ahead. 'Maybe not. Maybe not,' she thought, but the cold truth lay before her. 'Fred can't bother with supplies now. He must get the doctor.'

Fred was putting on his heavy coat while Anna fetched another muffler to wrap around his face. "After you're hitched, stop at the sideyard so I'll know when you leave." Anna watched from her kitchen window as Fred cautiously made his way to the barn, slipping occasionally, lap robe under his arm. She strained her eyes to see him pick up a large rock and chip the ice from the door lock, then he disappeared into the barn.

She quietly climbed the stairs to Elly's room where the child still slept fitfully, face flushed. Emma and her sister Frieda opened the door of their bedroom. "How is Elly?" they whispered.

"She's fine. Go back to sleep. It's very early." Wearily Anna trudged back downstairs to prepare breakfast for her sons. Time passed slowly, even though she was very busy.

The boys had a hard time with the chores. After milking, they had slipped on the ice while carrying the bucket, and little had been salvaged. The horses couldn't be brought to the water tank because the barnyard was a sheet of ice, so several pails had to be pumped and carried to the big drafters. It seemed they would drink the well dry. The cows were kinder, and their thirst quenched much sooner. After throwing down hay from the loft and spreading fresh straw in the stalls, the boys felt the livestock seemed content to spend the day in the confines of their home. Even though the barn was cold because of the dangerously low temperature outside, nature had given them the instinct to huddle with their own kind and benefit from the body heat emitted as their stalls grew steamy and warm.

The chickens were another matter. Grain had been

carried and spread in their trough. Water had been carried in a bucket that would now serve as the egg basket, but the chickens wanted out. Unaware of the situation outside, they dodged around the boys' feet trying to escape. Shavings, straw, and dust were kicked about. The big rooster crowed and flapped his wings in protest while the hens squawked and flew around in fright. After the eggs were gathered, the youngsters backed carefully out the door and quickly closed the latch, anxious to be away from the turmoil inside; but they were also thinking of the return trip they must make before nightfall to repeat the whole procedure. Perhaps Poppa could go with them.

Anna was up in Elly's room. She was awake now. The rash was much more pronounced, but the fever seemed no worse. Emma, who had arisen early because she was unable to sleep, helped Momma chip ice from a shallow pan. Anna had the idea to place a pan of water outside, knowing it would freeze quickly. The chips would be spoon fed to Elly to soothe her angry, red throat. The other children liked the idea and quickly put their own pan of water out to freeze. Ice was a rare treat, and it was fun to eat the crunchy stuff from a bowl, sometimes with sugar. It was nine o'clock and there was no sign of Fred.

Outside it was as though the whole world lay asleep. Nothing, no one, moved. Anna looked from every window. Only a fool would be out today if not necessary. The children were whining and bickering. "Stop! Your sister is sick upstairs."

"Momma, we won't have to stay in like last year, will we?" one or the children asked.

"Hush, the doctor will be here soon." Having heard the dreaded question put to her, Anna's head pounded as feelings of futility, yet hope, mounted inside her. She gave the children simple chores to do. The kitchen was the main living area in the home. The other rooms were closed off because of the cold. Girls were to sweep the floor and dust everything they could reach. "No climbing!" The boys would wash and dry the chimneys of the lamps she had set out. "No breaking! Even though a doctor's coming, we want no cuts or bruises." Also, the boys could polish Poppa's Sunday shoes. They needed to be kept busy. *How will I manage to do this again? Maybe it's something else. Something that doesn't amount to anything.*

Anna sat on the edge of Elly's bed. "What can Momma get you to eat?" The glassy eyed Elly only turned her head from side to side, and reached for her Momma's hand. Anna held the little hand that was so warm, but soon tucked it back under the blankets.

"You must keep covered so the fever will break. Are you ready for more ice?" The child nodded weakly and opened her mouth.

The children were doing their chores downstairs. She could hear them moving about, sometimes laughing, sometimes arguing. "Momma, where is Poppa?"

"Poppa went to get the doctor, he'll be here soon." With that Elly began to cry. Fear showed in her little face.

"No, no, he'll make you all better. Remember last time he was here? Soon after you started to get well." She's a year older, Anna thought. She remembers how it was.

"But why must I be sick again?"

Once more great tears poured down her face. Anna wiped them with her blue floral handkerchief and softly sang songs until the child wore herself out and slept. The cold bored into Anna's bones as she sat silently so as not to awaken her child. *Fred, Fred. Please hurry and be safe.* The clock chimed. She had lost track of the time. Anna counted. *Eleven! Good Lord. He's been gone so long. Something has happened.* Her stomach churned and growled. She'd had no breakfast. One had no appetite at a time like that.

There was a commotion downstairs. She started to run to the kitchen to quiet her brood. "Momma, Momma! Poppa is here. He has brought the doctor with him." Anna leaned against the wall for support. The relief overwhelmed her. Down the stairs on wobbly legs she trod. Yes, there they were. The doctor was climbing from the buggy. Fred was driving to the barn. The children were excited, and yet frightened. They were screechy and giggly, hiding under the table, punching each other. Anna reached for her bread spoon and rapped it on the table. "Enough!" And the children immediately fell silent and sat down to await the visitor's entrance.

There was something invasive yet majestic about a doctor's visit in your home. He held the answers. What would the answers be? The first time, it had seemed to Anna he held the power to proclaim life or death for her daughter as she stood breathlessly watching. But no, this was just a man, a man who had gone someplace far away from her little farm and learned from a book things she would never know. It was The Almighty who had the power.

It seemed to take forever for the doctor to make his way from the barnyard to the back step. Wordlessly, Anna held the door open, and the gentleman set his bag on the floor and removed his heavy clothing. Two steaming cups of coffee were poured and placed on the table by the time Fred trudged through the doorway. He looked exhausted. His face glowed a bright red from the cold, and his eyes were bloodshot from loss of sleep and the hours of driving in a bright sun over an ice encrusted countryside. Questions about the trip could be answered later. Anna set warm bread and butter before the men, and they ate and drank with stiff, cold fingers.

"Now then, tell me about Elly. How is she since Fred left this morning?"

Anna described her condition and what had transpired in recent hours as she refilled the cups.

"Anna, you do not look well yourself. Have you eaten?" questioned the doctor.

"I can't."

"You must. Emma, bring your Mother a plate and cup."

Emma quickly jumped to her feet, frightened of the man with the dark eyes, but also pleased to be called upon by him to serve Momma. Anna stuffed bread and butter into a dry mouth, but was surprised at how good the coffee tasted and how it warmed her through. Then the doctor arose and said, "Let us go tend to our little one."

The trio climbed the steps reenacting a scene that had taken place a year ago. *Am I dreaming?* Anna thought. *We just did all this. It's all the same.* She looked at Fred's broad back as he went before her. 'Poor Fred. Poor dear man.' And as they reached the top she could not help but reach out and touch his shoulder. He turned, looking surprised, and took her hand and led her to the bed where their sleeping child lie.

The doctor quietly placed his bag on the blue and rose floral carpet. Placing his fingers over his lips, he stood silently and studied. Finally, he blew out a deep breath and moved close to the bed. He lightly tickled Elly under her

43

chin. The drowsy child focused her eyes and seemed to accept the fact that the doctor was here and would help her. Softly asking questions, he began the examination that would reveal the nature of the illness. Would the revelation bring joy or sorrow? Anna stood close to the corner of the room and twisted the buttons on her dress. Many years from now, this same nervous habit would be repeated in another bedroom where Elly lie as an adult, suffering from the sickness that would finally take her life.

"Elly, may I see your tongue?" the doctor queried. Observing the bright red appearance, the swelling and tiny pits, all the symptoms of a 'strawberry tongue'; the bright red spots spreading over the neck and chest, the fever, together with the problems she had endured through the night, there was no doubt in his mind. Amazing! He'd never seen a patient infected twice. Especially a year apart. He'd heard of cases, but it was quite rare. *Could I have misdiagnosed the last time?* No! No, this was definitely Scarlet Fever. Clear and obvious. He buttoned the child's gown and covered her.

"Elly's such a good girl. Do you want me to leave you alone now?" he smiled at the youngster. Elly nodded 'yes' and looked to Momma. "Remember the tiny box of pills I gave you last time? I have some more for you and they'll help you feel better." With that, he took his bag and beckoned Anna and Fred into the hall.

Their eyes were wide, and they were breathless, wanting to hear, but not wanting to, also. "It's as we thought. It's Scarlet Fever again. I'm sure of it."

"But how?" Anna started.

"I don't know. I just don't know. I wish there was something else I could say or do. For now, just do as you've been doing. Give her these pills as before. You know that I have to contact the supervisor. He won't be out in this

44

weather, but you know what you must do. I'm sorry. Anna, try to get some rest. I'll be back in a couple of days to check on her. Fred, shall we try to make it back to town?"

Anna didn't go downstairs. She went to her bedroom to watch out the window. She pulled back the lace curtain and stared at the whitened world. Finally, she saw Fred pull the buggy to the gate and the doctor cautiously make his way along the icy path and climb in. As they drove off, she didn't move. She felt as frozen as the world around her. Anna couldn't remember the last time she had cried. She really couldn't remember. But now something was happening. She fell across the bed and great sobs racked her body. She buried her face in the quilt to smother them, but her shoulders heaved and her tears poured forth and her fingers dug deep into the bedding. She cried for little Elly, for her other children, for her dear husband, for herself, and, it seemed, she cried for the whole world. Finally, exhausted, she turned on her back and stared at the ceiling.

"Momma? Momma?" The children downstairs were calling. They assumed her to be with Elly. She pulled herself to her feet and wiped her face with her hanky. Tiptoeing to Elly's door, she was pleased to see her asleep. There was water in a pitcher on the dresser. Pouring a little on her handkerchief, she washed her hot, tear stained face, repinned her hair, and calmly descended the stairs to inform her children of what lay ahead.

9

Coming back to the present, Anna stirred in her rocker. She was tired and felt as though she had been through a terrible ordeal. *What time was it?* Good. Emma was still there. She was whistling in the kitchen. The windows were opened slightly, and Anna was aware of a soft, warm outdoor freshness filling the house. *It will soon be winter.* The thought chilled her. *Why did it always seem there were more winters than summers? I guess because we were always so busy in the summer, they went by so quickly. So much to do.* Her mind seemed to spin as she sat and envisioned the many chores she had performed during her farm years. She saw herself making lye soap, pouring the mixture of lard and lye into the large granite pan. Early the next morning she would hurry outside to cut it into the neat squares that would be used to wash the clothes, and even the dishes. The big batch would usually last her all year.

Anna's hands slightly opened and closed as she remembered the many batches of bread dough she had kneaded, the many kuchens and rolls she had baked. *Wednesday. I think Wednesday was baking day. Winter and Summer. No matter how hot.* She fondly remembered Winter Wednesdays when the aroma filled the whole house. The warmth, the anticipation of her baked goods being taken from the oven, the special excitement of the family when she would take the pie receiver from the hook on the wall and deliver the golden pies from the cook stove to the table, all filled Anna with a sense of pride. These were her gems, this was her art, something she knew she did well.

"Momma, it looks so nice and smells so good!"

"Nonsense. Anyone could do it."

Wash day. Monday. She tried to push the thought away. Anna's hands would be red and sometimes bleeding from the wash water and cold weather. Trying to dry clothes in winter was a chore. She would hang the clothes on the line just as late into the year as she could. All too soon the cold weather froze the clothes so stiff she would bring them inside and stand them against the wall to thaw. Although the children thought this sight was quite entertaining, it was time to give up the clothes line and start drying them indoors. Draped over chairs and other odds and ends the clothes would dry from the heat of the house. And oh, the ironing was never done it seemed. Until the girls got bigger, this was a chore she had to perform herself. With seven in the family, it turned into an all day job, sometimes more. It was a much easier task in the winter, for the cook stove had to be burning constantly to heat the plates that clamped onto the iron. Two iron plates were placed on the stove, and when hot, one was clamped onto the iron. Anna would iron until the plate cooled, then she traded it for the heated counterpart, and the cool plate was placed back onto the stove to reheat. The fabric was usually harsh and the iron heavy, but her arm was strong. It took great dexterity and judgment to determine the temperature for the different goods in the work pants and the dainty home sewn blouses. Many years ago, as a young lass, Anna had scorched a thing or two while learning to iron. She

47

would try not to be as harsh and critical on her daughters as Momma had been to her.

Again a soft breeze wafted through the window. She rocked slowly. It was warm but not hot like it usually was for this time of year. Anna could smell Autumn creeping in sleepily to overtake summer. Yes, she could always, since a little girl, smell the seasons. She remembered standing in the yard when just a few patches of green were winking at her here and there amongst the mud and the last little pillows of snow. She'd close her eyes tightly and sniff. There it was! "Momma, Momma! Spring is here!" How Momma would chuckle. "Anna, Anna. So you can tell us the seasons like a calendar." And Anna felt somewhat foolish, but deep inside something told her that when her favorite season unceremoniously arrived she would know.

THE END OF AUGUST

10

The end of August always brought a change in her life. An ending of things. Of summer. As a child it meant the end of being home with family, playing hard, and working hard with no schedule of any kind. It was time to think about starting school once more, and when Anna's own children would again trek down the gravel road to their little school house two miles away, there was an extreme sense of sadness and yet freedom. How quiet it was! How she missed their help, yet she seemed to accomplish so much. The Autumn fruits of her garden were ready to be preserved in jars. The relishes, pickles, and tomatoes on the shelves brought her menagerie of canned goods full circle, completing what had been started the season before.

One morning Anna took a pan of tomato peelings to toss over the fence to her chickens. How they flocked to, and fought over, the juicy morsels. She forgot about demanding chores in the house and laced her fingers through the wire fence and laughed aloud as the hens snatched coveted pieces from each others beaks. It was close to noon, and now she must go fix dinner for Fred. It was so easy, cooking for two. But instead of going to the house, she sat on a log that lay under the mulberry trees.

The weather was perfect: dry, with a hint of a breeze touching her cheek. A very melancholy feeling came over her. It always did at this time of year. Sleepy, sad. It was so quiet. It seemed the countryside was getting ready for a long, long sleep, and would soon cover itself with a majestic colored quilt. For some reason, these Autumn days always made her lonesome for her childhood, for her school friends. She had rarely seen other children except at school, and she thought now of the long walk to and from the tiny room where she had spent many happy, and sometimes a few unpleasant, hours. Smiling to herself, she recalled walking home one particular afternoon. As usual, the boys were frisky, and teasing the girls. Finally, Anna had her fill. She took her tin dinner pail and whomped her tormentor over the head. The stunned lad was unhurt, but henceforth had great respect for Anna. Feeling victorious and smug, she was the heroine of her little friends, but when Anna had to explain the dent in her dinner pail to Momma, a stern lecture followed. Poppa had been sitting in his wooden chair, tilted back, resting against the wall as was his usual manner. As the child turned, tears stinging her eyes, he gave her a proud wink. The tears dried, and once more Poppa had made everything OK.

Even now, still sitting under the mulberry tree, she missed him. Poppa had been gone several years now, and much to her dismay, Anna could scarcely remember what he looked like. She wanted to remember him in his younger years, strong, able, her protector; but the memory freshest and foremost in her mind was the dreadful accident that had taken place on that cold terrible day so long ago. That was the face she saw. Drawn with pain. That was the body she remembered. Limp and helpless. *And the eyes, as he lie in bed as his life slowly drained from him. His eyes.* There was a sort of pleading, mingled with fear and despair. Anna sensed a look of contrition. He seemed to say, 'I'm so sorry. I didn't want to do this to you.' And she had fought the rage within her, to not be able to make everything good for Poppa as he had always made it for her.

Now Anna shook her head and rubbed her eyes so the bad memory would go away. At least Momma was still here. Sometimes, though, late at night, she would tip toe into her parlor and stare at the big picture of Poppa that hung so majestically over the side board and she would talk to him.

"I wish you could see my children. I gave my firstborn your name. You never even got to meet my husband. You'd like him. He's a good man. Kind, gentle and quiet. I do so love my children and husband." Anna would marvel at how easy it was to tell Poppa all these things, but so difficult to tell anyone else.

Then once again, Anna opened the drawer to the side board and pulled out the atlas. She had turned to the same story so many times the big book always fell open to the precise page. Among countless maps and articles about other people, there it would be: Poppa's story. It had been written in 1877, even before she was born. 'Phillip Weyhrich,' it started. Even though Poppa's name was Johann Phillip, he had been called Phillip since she could remember. She traced the lines with her finger and proudly read.

PHILLIP WEYHRICH, the subject of our sketch, was born in Germany in 1834, and emigrated to the United States in 1852, and located in Tazewell county, where he labored by the month on farms and whatever he could get to do, until 1857, when, after carefully saving his hard earned wages, he was able to enter one hundred acres of good land in Sand Prairie township, and commenced to break prairie and improve a farm. In the same year(1857) he married Miss Elizabeth Shaffer, daughter of John and Elizabeth Shaffer. She was born in Sand Prairie township, Tazewell county, in 1842. Immediately after their marriage Mr. Weyhrich moved his wife to his farm, where he had prepared a comfortable home, and energetically engaged in farming and raising stock.

Mr. Weyhrich commenced his course in life a very poor man, and had nothing for his dependence but his labor and his good name; but through a course of steady and untiring labor, good economy, and fair dealing with his fellow men, he soon began to prosper, and with the assistance of his industrious and enterprising wife, has thus far made life a success. He is of energetic and enterprising habits, and is at all times willing to do his full share to aid and assist all useful enterprises that will benefit the country. He is held in high esteem for his good citizenship, and has many warm friends. He is now the father of five children, one son and four daughters; one child is dead and four living, for all of whom he cherishes the warmest affection.

"Warmest affection"...she liked that. She had thrived and flourished on Poppa's affection. His baby. Anna pondered Poppa's hard life in his early years. He had come from Hesse Darmstadt alone and penniless, and found his way to Illinois. Working for pennies a month as a hired hand, he sometimes had to live in the barn and wear hand-me-downs from his employer, but the day came when he climbed into his buggy and set out to buy his very own farm. He succeeded. After that, there were more farms, not large, but his own, so that, at the time of his death, Johann Phillip Weyhrich was a prominent figure. A special train had run from Pekin to Green Valley so that local dignitaries could attend his funeral.

Anna's fingers picked up the yellowed clipping from the Peoria Star newspaper dated January, 1899. It read:

'BIG FUNERAL. The funeral of Phillip Weyhrich, of Sand Prairie, was largely attended yesterday, there being a great number from here present. A special train was run from Pekin. The funeral took place from the family residence at Sand Prairie. The Rev. Krietmeyer delivered the funeral eulogy, after which the cortege proceeded to the cemetery. They were met at Sand Prairie by the Pekin delegation. The deceased had a wide acquaintance and his death is lamented by all those who knew him. In his youth he encountered all those difficulties and sacrifices which lie in the way of self development and self promotion. In his last days he was able to enjoy the fruits of his early labors.

He was a good man and gained the respect of many people. The family who survive can ill afford to lose him, and their grief is great in this hour of sorrow. Sympathy is being expressed for them on all sides. Among those who went from Pekin yesterday were Louis Zinzer, Anderson Meyers, Henry Reuling, Jacob Roelfs, Julius Jaeckel, Carl Winkel, Dr. Bailey, Mayor Sapp, H. Schnellbacher, George Grimm, H. Weyrich, Peter Steinmetz, J. Meyers and many others.'

So the saga was ended. The man, larger than life, had left his mark in time, leaving a legacy that his descendants would only hear and read about.

11

Anna's Momma had borne nine babies. Her second, a girl, lived only a short time, and the baby boy, Nickolas, that had been born only a year before Anna, in 1879, was also taken from them. Many had lost their infants, but even more tragic was the number of mothers struck down at a young age leaving large families that needed tending and nurturing. Lacking in knowledge to counter illness and disease, with a minimum of the necessities for survival, life was difficult for even the strongest.

Such a thing had happened to Poppa's brother George. Anna had been not quite nine, but she could remember as if it were yesterday. Uncle George and his wife Eliazbeth had had a large family. Four children had died young. Six years earlier, Auntie had given birth to twins. Baby Margaret was born on October 31 and a boy was born on November 1. Margaret thrived, but the boy died shortly after birth. Now Auntie was going to have another baby. Anna was old enough now to help with her baby cousin and looked forward to the new arrival. Momma had promised her that they would visit as soon as the baby came. The long months of waiting were almost over and Anna had imagined herself rocking the baby while Momma helped with the many chores that awaited.

One night Anna had overheard Momma share her
concern with Poppa. She was worried about Auntie
Elizabeth. "After all, she's forty seven years old. This will be
her fourteenth child." Momma went on and on about
Auntie's well being, how frail she seemed, and how she
wished the babe was here and it was all over for her. Of
course there would be help from the older girls at home, but
still, there were so many in the household to be cared for.
The eldest daughter, Elizabeth, had been married early in the
year and was expecting her first born, so Auntie Elizabeth
would be a new mother and a new grandmother all in the
same year. How exciting!

But then news came that the baby was stillborn. It was a
boy and Auntie had named him Emil. Anna wept. She felt
cheated. She had waited so long. Momma comforted her
and reminded her that Auntie Elizabeth's grandbaby would
be here in a few months. But that would be winter! At
Christmas time. They could not travel in winter like they
could now. It was almost summer, it was warm, and
Momma and she could easily travel the country roads alone.
Anna thought back to past winters. They would sometimes
be home for weeks. Anna wailed to Momma that the baby
would be 'old' before she would ever get to visit it.

But news of Baby Emil paled to the message that Uncle
Adam had brought two days later. Anna could still
remember the lovely June afternoon when Poppa's younger
brother rode hurriedly up the lane and jumped from his
buggy. She and her twelve year old brother George were at
the garden pulling weeds from the young beans and potatoes
that were shooting up so heartily. They quickly ran to greet
their uncle, ready to play some silly game with him. Adam
was funny and always had time to wrestle with the boys or

play a game of tag with Anna, but now he brushed right past them and told them to stay outside. Hurt and a little miffed, Anna and her brother busied themselves by pulling grass and foliage for Uncle Adam's horse. Anna braided it's foretop and wished she had a pretty ribbon to fasten it. Suddenly the children were startled by a loud crying from the house. Looking at one another, they warily walked towards the back door and waited. Before long, Uncle Adam, looking not like himself, rushed past them. Anna could wait no longer. Rushing inside, she saw Momma's anguished face. "What is it?"

Momma couldn't answer for a long time. Finally, she spoke quietly. "Aunt Elizabeth is dead. She went to be with her baby." Anna ran to Poppa. She felt afraid. Only Poppa could hold her and shield her at a time like this. He was strong and not crying.

When Anna was taken to her uncle's home the next night, and she was led to see her Auntie lying dead, a horrible numbness came over her. The usual happy, unrestrained household had become a place of mourning and despair. She couldn't talk to her cousins, could hardly look at them. Everyone seemed a stranger. These beloved kin, her family, all took on the appearance of grieving, distant strangers.

Someone offered her something to eat. She refused. "Poppa, may we go home?" Poppa put his arm around her and nodded his head. That night in bed Anna had horrible dreams of her own Momma leaving her, and she cried for Aunt Elizabeth and knew how much she would miss her.

12

Anna wondered how long she had been sitting under the Mulberry tree. Hoisting herself to her feet, she started for the house. One did not sit around daydreaming when there was so much to do. The afternoons went by so quickly. Today she would bring down all the feather beds and air them in the sunshine. Packed away all summer, it wouldn't be long until they were a welcome addition to the beds. On cold winter nights, one could snuggle deeply into the down and feel as cozy and content as a kitten nestled in mounds of straw in the manger of the big barn.

It took a long time to unpack the feather beds and carry them downstairs, and she wished the children were there to help. When she finally finished, Anna was weary and longed to rest. But now it was late afternoon, and she would watch the road to be sure her children were in sight. This summer there had been gypsies. More than once. The children were always the first to hear them. Running to the house, flushed with excitement, they would proclaim the approach of the fearsome, yet mysterious caravans. Fred was usually in the fields when they came, but he'd always warn not to let them water their horses from the water tank, lest some disease be carried from another source. As the horses pulled the

timeworn wagons into the lot, Anna would quickly gather
what she could from her kitchen, bread and such, so that
when the knock sounded at the back door she could deftly
open it a crack and slip it into the eager hand with no words
exchanged.

One afternoon she and the girls had been hard at work in
the garden when the clamor in the barnyard brought her to
her feet. Knowing full well they could not reach the house in
time, Anna calmly walked to meet the dark stranger that
approached. Her mind whirling, she pointed to the smoke
house where the remains of some unused meat hung, made
rancid by the summer heat. The man entered the smoke
house and reappeared with his find, grateful, ready to share
the bounty with family and friends. Anna felt terrible. She
had so much. Still, a wave of anger swept over her. She and
Fred worked so hard for what they had. Her sympathy went
to the women, and especially the children. The beautiful
dark eyed, dark haired children.

Farm children were usually yearning for new playmates
and friends, someone aside from brothers, sisters, and
parents. Someone with a new game to play, a cherished doll
to hug, a story to tell. Therefore, when little Elly spied the
girl standing by the wagon wheel, a girl just her size, looking
shy and intimidated, she pulled her hand from her Mother's
grasp and ran to the waif. With a child's abandon and
innocence she thrust her beloved rag doll into the thin little
arms of the gypsy child. Chaos prevailed. Anna ran
screaming her daughter's name. The gypsy mother was
momentarily stunned. She too had been standing by the
wagon to stretch her back and legs. The wagon was most
uncomfortable, but now it was parked under a wonderful
sheltering tree that gave relief from the parching sun. Both
mothers reached their daughters at the same time. Each

58

hoisted their baby to their hip and they looked at each other. Breathless. The dark eyes of one who had no roots, called a wagon her home, knew not where she and her family would sleep tonight, looked into the blue eyes of one whose roots were deeply entrenched in the sandy soil on which she stood, one who had never traveled further than her own little prairie community. But there was a fleeting bond. A moment passed between them that made them sisters. Their babies. The instinct to protect and shield. And not a word was spoken. Then the young woman whispered into her daughter's ear, and the little one obediently placed the doll back into Elly's arms.

Anna wondered about this woman. Was she happy? Did she have parents? Where had this child that she held been born? The need to give her something embraced Anna and she instinctively reached into her apron pocket. Nothing except the damp hankie she had used to wipe her brow while in the garden. "Wait, please. Wait here."

Still carrying Elly and beckoning her other youngsters into the house, Anna hurried to the sideboard in the parlor. Opening the drawer she nervously fumbled through a small array of personal treasures. Her 'happy things' she liked to call them. After only a moment she knew. Her fingers lifted up the snowy white handkerchief with the tatted lace and the perfectly shaped heart sewn into one corner. The one Momma had so painstakingly worked on and presented to her one Christmas. Anna raced outside to see that no one in the band of gypsies had moved. Slowing her pace, she approached them. Feeling somewhat embarrassed, she pressed the cherished hankie into the sun-darkened hand of the young woman. Still clasping hands, Anna, not knowing what to say, whispered "God bless you." She then turned and ran into the house, her heart pounding from the emotions she was feeling.

Now summer was over, and the gypsies probably would not be back until the next. She could see her children happily and safely skipping down the dusty road towards home. The feather beds that were strewn across the front porch railing could now be turned over so that the sun could bake deeply into the colorful ticking. After supper Anna and her youngsters would bring them inside and stack them in the spare room till winter's use, the freshness filling the air for days.

13

Fred was in the pasture breaking in the offspring of his bay mare. He had gingerly harnessed her and hitched her to a hayrack. Anna had warned him to wait until the boys were home to help. "Get a little rest this afternoon."

Early that morning he had asked if she would like rabbit for supper. "Yes, that sounds good." And so off he had gone, not for the sole purpose of bringing home meat for the table, but also because he loved to roam the fields, especially the banks of the Mackinaw River. As he stayed alert for wild game, his eyes looked keenly at the earth before his feet. Many times he had been rewarded for his intense searching. Suddenly there it would be! Sometimes half buried, sometimes fully exposed, glinting in the sun, beckoning to be picked up and polished was another Indian arrow head! Fred would laugh and exclaim his delight aloud, as if someone were at his side to share his thrilling find. As he wiped away the dirt that had hidden the stone for so many years and rubbed it on his pant leg till it shone, a very somber feeling would come over him. He held a part of history. No other hands had touched this arrow since the one who had last released it. Was he, too, hunting food for his family's supper? How many years ago had this person trod the same ground where Fred now stood? High on the bluff of the river he would gaze across the wild grasses and envision the settlement: a tranquil place with women working together while talking and laughing softly; horses, sleek and muscular, ready to carry their rider across the prairies where they could roam for days without sight of another human. Now Fred could feel the presence of his hunting companion and walk with him as he approached his camp where white smoke arose against a cloudless blue sky. He saw the hunter's children run to meet their father. Fred dropped the arrowhead into his pocket and left them, walking across the golden fields toward home.

Anna was in her kitchen. There would be a feast at the supper table tonight, because, as always, the hunt had proven productive. She was thankful for the bounty that the prairie provided her and her family. A crashing sound came from outside, pulling her from her reverie. Peering out the window, she saw a most unwelcome sight, one that every farm family was loathe to think about. A runaway! The young horse was wildly pulling the hayrack around the barnyard, out of control, being whipped into a frenzy by the beating reins.

Anna ran outside. "Fred! Fred!" The poor animal, wild-eyed, careened crazily, slamming the rack into the fence and scattering a flock of chickens as it tried to rid itself of the foreign thing that was causing its bondage. "Stay! Whoa!" Anna hollered until her throat went dry and the dust caused her to cough, bent in dizziness. Finally she heard more shouts. Fred! He had raced across the field and was in the barn lot. Dodging. Chasing. Now that the animal was tiring, he finally was able to grab hold and slowly pace the colt to a halt. It took a long while to calm the trembling creature. Together, the two unhitched the harness and Fred examined closely to see if any wounds were present. Miraculously, other than a few scrapes and nicks, the horse seemed to be stable. Not so with the hayrack, and everything with which it had made destructive contact.

For the rest of the afternoon and well into the evening, the sounds of hammers and saws could be heard, correcting fences and wheels, buildings and gates. Fred and the boys made sure the now stabled animal was calm and feeding on the sweet clover and secret nibbles of sugar the girls had sneaked from Momma's pantry. The clang of the dinner bell broke the air, and Anna walked to Fred and put a beckoning hand on his tired shoulder. "Come. Eat the rabbit. I made it just the way you like it. Brown and crispy."

14

So the autumn went, and it was soon to be Thanksgiving. It had been an uneventful time, save for one episode Anna was quite happy to see end. Little Henry was missing! The duck that Emma, Elly, and Frieda had made into a pet over the summer, had suddenly not shown up one Monday morning for feeding time. The search was on. They were calling, coaxing, climbing, and looking in the most likely and unlikely places a child could imagine. As school time approached with no sign of Little Henry, it was obvious the hunt would be delayed until afternoon. When afternoon finally came, the walk, or the run, home from school had seemed to last forever. The dirt road loomed long and endless ahead and seemed to be swallowed up into the horizon. Several times the three lasses had to plunk down alongside the grassy ditch to catch their breath. Little Elly had assured them she was feeling fine and was quite able to keep up with her two sisters. Finally the wide welcome driveway was in sight. A dash to the front porch where Little Henry liked to bask in the afternoon sun brought a wash of disappointment. "Momma! Momma! Is he here? Did you find him?" When Momma replied in the negative, little hearts sank, and again rounds were made in search of the elusive duckling. At bedtime, when three weary girls climbed into bed, questions and pleadings pounded Anna's ears.

"Where could Little Henry be? Why would he leave? What evil animal could have snatched him? Could they stay home from school tomorrow to further the search?" Anna wearily sat on the bed and listened to extra long prayers, and was sorry she had ever heard of a duck called Little Henry.

Over the next few days things did not change. It became a ritual, the morning and evening pursuit, but an unsuccessful one. By Friday the girls had begun to accept the fact their web-footed friend was forever gone, and on Saturday morning they turned their thoughts and energies to merriment and mirth. After a lively game of tag, the three had carried dolls and blankets to the front yard and spread out their imaginary house under the shade of a towering tree. As baby dolls were being fed and bedded, a strange sound wafted from the field across the road. All three heard it. Leaving their fancied home and their play things, they raced across the dirt road into the field to find the source of the calling sounds. Closer and closer it came, and suddenly before their very eyes stood their beloved pet, stretching his neck and squawking his objections to this strange scene that had been his home these last few days.

"Henry! Little Henry!" Six small hands engulfed Henry with pets and strokes and his little head fairly bobbed as the three ran home with their long lost treasure.

15

Thanksgiving morning broke bright and sunny.
Although a deep snow covered the countryside, the weather
had been mild. Anna stood by the window of the cold
bedroom and let the rays shine on her back. The day before
had been spent baking pies and preparing special dishes for
today. Now she must hurry downstairs and prepare the big
pork roast that had been saved from a recent butchering day,
a day especially set aside to garner meat for corn picking
time. Fred and his sons had been in the fields long hours and
had little time for anything else. Plenty of pork was on hand
to serve to the weary workers when they would trudge to the
house for their sporadic dinners and suppers. It seemed a
perpetual meal had been spread across her table that picking
season, but now the white table linen was in place and dishes
that were seldom used graced the table on this day set aside
to give special thanks. The bowl with the purple grapes
painted in the bottom would, as always, hold plums Anna
had preserved, and the one with the red cherries hanging
from a stem with the soft pink blossoms surrounding it
would contain her applesauce. The big bowl with the gold
lacy trim would be filled with a mountain of mashed potatoes
and be placed beside the matching meat platter.

"Momma, will the man come to the door again?"

Anna frowned. "Probably not." The child was referring to the tramp that had paid a visit during dinner the past three years—not the same person, of course. It was a known fact that tramps, as they were called, left marks denoting which house was known to give a small gift of food. "Just in case," she noted as she set aside an assortment of food stuffs in a small box. Sure enough, as Anna was dishing out dessert, a meek knock was heard at the door. Little Elly promptly slipped from her chair and hid under the table. The two older girls ran to Poppa, and the boys sat quietly.

"Sit down and hush!" Fred commanded. Cautiously, Anna opened the door. Wordlessly, eyes straight ahead, she went for the little box and swiftly handed it over to the visitor.

"Bless you," the man mumbled and was gone. The family relaxed. Elly returned to her seat, but the whys and wherefores of such a man and others like him arose from the children, upsetting the festivities and causing duress. Fred spoke calmly. "Children, listen to me. Now listen. Remember the day! We have so much. Some do not. It is an honor the Lord has chosen us to share with someone who has nothing. And please to remember the man in your prayers tonight."

"Yes Poppa."

"Now," boomed Fred, "let's have Momma's pie."

16

Soon it was to be Christmas. No one made much to-do about the season. Anna did some baking for Christmas morning: Leb Kuchen, Springerlies, and Pfeppernuts. But the event that was most awaited, the closest to Anna's heart, was Christmas Eve. For weeks she had toiled to complete the Christmas dresses for her three daughters, and she feared the boys would outgrow their shirts before she could finish them. Now it was here. After an early supper, the children would take their chairs into the parlor and place them in a row. Then each took a piece of paper, wrote their name on it and placed it on their respective chair. In the early morning the five would hurry down the stairs to find perhaps a doll, a hand hewn wooden animal, a wagon, and one special year, doll buggies for the girls. A sweater, and a bag filled with candy and an orange were traditional and expected gifts.

One particular Christmas Eve stayed in Anna's mind always. Fred was an elder at church and it was his duty to light the candles on the Christmas tree at the beginning of the service. She could not remember a time when the heavens didn't open to yield a sprinkling, sometimes a vast, amount of snow on this Holy Night. The ride in the surrey had seemed magical. She and Fred in the front, the two little ones on small chairs in the middle, and Emma and the boys in the back. Yes, it had been cold and dark, but the blankets were warm, and the lanterns emitted a golden glow to show the way. The snow flakes fell softly and had never seemed bigger. There were no sounds, save the horses hooves and the surrey wheels crunching the snow.

The arrival at church was a scene to behold! Rows and rows of buggies and surreys, lanterns still aglow, casting light, making shadows. Gentlemen were helping their ladies' descent. Mothers were lifting their children to the snow covered ground. Fathers were blanketing horses that would wait, heads bowed. There was a hurried trek across the church yard, and when the doors were opened, they saw a breathtaking transformation had occurred in the little church.

Greenery adorned the windows, the altar, the doors. And candles! Anna had never seen so many, twinkling, beckoning, warming...giving a glow that made the parishioners feel they were entering heaven itself. There in the corner, right up front, was the tree! The very tree, clipped full of candles that Fred would have the honor of lighting. Anna looked at the people, most her kin, their faces rose red from the cold, but also flushed with the excitement and meaning of this night. Both parents' and children's eyes shone brightly as they took their seats, embraced, shook hands, and wished a blessed Christmas.

Anna and her family sat in the front. Her sons had been chosen to pump the organ and would take turns to pump the air so the organ, played by the sisters Volk, could accompany the people as they sweetly proclaimed their joy through music. After the first hymn, the minister nodded, and Fred arose and took up the long handled pole and approached the tree, proceeding to light the many candles. Children stood on tiptoe to see the act, and men craned their necks around

ladies' large hats to catch a glimpse. Anna, not wanting to
appear proud or smug, mostly looked at her lap. Finally,
when the last of the candles was lighted and Fred stepped
away, a low sigh was heard throughout. The tree was a
golden spire, illuminating the church and causing hundreds
of shapes and forms to dance on the walls and ceiling.

Anna's heart swelled with pride as she watched her
husband return to his seat. She saw her sons sitting so erect
and still next to the organ. As she looked down at her three
young daughters beside her, Emma looked up and smiled,
showing the deep dimple in her right cheek. "My God," she
thought, "I do have a beautiful family!" Now she and her
fellow church people were filled with Christmas, and with
the lights, and the music, and with love.

All too soon, little ones were being bundled up, some
already lulled to sleep by the music, the glow, and the
warmth. Older ones were eager for the trip home, the sooner
to get to sleep and awaken to a new toy or treat and, surely, a
sack of candy.

17

The sun had moved and was casting a glow on the peach dining room wall. Once more Anna was awake and let her eyes rest on nothing specific. She removed her glasses and produced a handkerchief from her pocket. After wiping and wiping, she peered through the lens only to repeat the procedure. Finally, accepting the fact her glasses were clean she thought, 'It's just my eyes. What can I expect at my age?' But she wanted to see clearly! Does anyone, no matter how old or decrepit the body may be, not want to still see, or to hear, to have all their reasons and senses sharp and clear?

Until just a few years ago, she would awaken at night and, with a sleep hazed mind, try to remember how old she was. When reality would come, she'd stiffen and burrow deep under the covers as if to escape the truth. She liked to work hard, keep busy. She'd always had to. There was still the drive and energy within, but now it was trapped in a body that couldn't accommodate the release of these inner abilities. So with time came acceptance. She was old. She would accept help. In fact, she now welcomed it. *I'm in my own home. I am fortunate.* But sometimes still, rebellion roared inside her. It screamed and prodded. *I want to be out! I want strong legs to walk across a freshly plowed field, to smell the dirt. I want to have Fred sweep me up and carry me across the creek so my long dress doesn't get wet. I want to gather eggs and smell the sweet straw as I nest my chicks. To braid a child's hair, to dance the polka on a Saturday night. Oh, to dance the polka, the music filling her head, turning and spinning as the onlookers smile and clap in time. Please, to do the polka once more.* And the desire would peak and cause her to tremble. But then she would plunge back to reality. The realization that these things were to be no more.

Acceptance had replaced anger not too long ago. Had it been a month, a year? Anna couldn't remember. Time blended itself into a blur now.

Emma had suggested a drive, a drive in the countryside. She had readily accepted, but that day, during the drive, Anna slowly noticed a change. Things were different. Everywhere they drove it was happening, or had happened. The farms, the homesteads, were taking on a ghost-like quality. New homes dotted the countryside, and only occasionally would one see a fine old farm house.

And rarely did one see a windmill. Only a few had been maintained or preserved. The rest were skeletal remains, some with only the tower standing, some with most of the blades missing, and the wheel almost bare.

Anna had loved the windmill. Some days when she felt tired or somewhat overwhelmed she would leave her kitchen and walk along the dusty path to the nearby towering frame. Leaning against the cool metal she would listen to the steady hum of the big wheel as the wind blew the silvery blades. It was comforting, this ever spinning, ever reliable apparatus. How well she could remember the many times after heavy rains, Fred would climb the tower to see if the rising river waters were flooding his farmland. The boys would beg to join Poppa—to climb so high and view the prairies from this lofty place. But no, Anna would not allow it. So she and the children would stand below and breathlessly watch as Fred deftly found his way to the top. And from there he would observe the encroaching waters and be prepared for any damage to his crops.

The windmill had been their life line, capturing the energy of air currents to operate the water pumps. Of course with the development of the gasoline engine and electricity, she knew they were no longer used or needed. Still, these giants once dotted the farm lands in vast numbers and it grieved her to see them destroyed or disregarded, relics that would soon be lost forever. Future generations would have only pictures to gaze upon and ask what they were used for.

Yes, the demise of the windmill saddened Anna, but nothing could compare to the distress she felt as she witnessed the passing of the old barns. She had listened one day as her granddaughter lamented the fact that the beautiful old barns were disappearing. Now she was seeing for herself. Had it happened so slowly and gradually that she had never noticed before?

Again and again Anna saw what once had been a majestic structure, now the product of neglect. Years of wind and rain stripped away paint and left haymow doors dangling, windows broken, gaping holes in roofs. Some had collapsed, and she winced as she imagined the once strong building, so painstakingly planned and put together with precision and skill. The barns had once stood tall and sound, pride of the farmer and haven for beast, an entity to be passed to future generations. But without care and maintenance the years took their toll, and the old buildings slowly and shamefully fell, like a once strong warrior reluctantly going down in defeat at the hands of his enemies.

" Take me to our first place." Her first place...Anna and Fred had lived on another farm, close to the little village of Tremont for the first two years of marriage. The home was a log house, rough and not pretty, but warm, full of love and their son was born there. It was miles from their families, though, so when the opportunity arose to acquire the farm close to Momma and to Fred's Poppa, they had been elated to go.

Now she had to go back. Emma headed the car east, down Townline Road. Reaching their destination, they pulled off the road and parked. Anna hadn't been there for a long time. A cozy newer home stood where her long ago log home had been. The trees and surrounding buildings were foreign. But there! There was the barn. As it was. It was painted and preserved. But it seemed smaller than she remembered.

"The barn was new when I came here as a bride. And Fred spent so much time there. He loved it." She could remember vividly watching Fred go to the barn to saddle the mare that hot August day so long past. She had stood at the window, her belly swollen, ready to release this encumbrance she had carried so many months. It was fore noon. He could bring the doctor quickly. Feeling faint and with sweat pouring down her face, Anna forced herself to stay at the window to wave her white handkerchief. With a wave, the pair galloped swiftly down the road and out of sight. Anna lay on the bed until their return, alone and frightened.

And that night, as a howling wind blew and lightning snapped and thunder clapped down around them, she delivered her first born, Albert Phillip. Could it have been so long ago?

She stood quietly beside Emma, not talking. Suddenly, there in the wide doorway of the barn she saw someone. Yes! It was Fred, his blue work shirt stretched tight across his

shoulders. Carrying two buckets. *Water for his calves.*
Smiling, she watched him. *He's his happiest doing this. Caring
for his livestock. His barn is his haven, his domain.* Fred
disappeared inside. Anna waited and waited. She blinked
hard. Then she realized. Realized it was not real. It was only
in her mind. But she had seen him! She had!

Now she turned to Emma and said, "I'm ready to go."
She had come full circle today. It was time to go back to her
city home, to sit in her rocker and let the memories flood
through her, to carry her away and to escape the present.

18

The hoe pulled dry dirt up around the potato plants and formed mounds to protect the leaves from a late day sun. It was May. It had been a rainy spring and her garden was late, but the weeds were thriving. Anna leaned on the hoe handle. She had considered having one of her little daughters do the task, but likely as not, precious plants would be chopped off, and that would not do. Now she was in pain. It had been with her for some time now, leaving, but coming back again. Some days gave glorious respite. Others, it was there like a foe, torturing her, causing her to be short with her family, restraining her from her duties. No one had noticed, but now she must confide. She would see a doctor. And after several consultations her fears were confirmed. "You have some sort of growth in your stomach. I don't know for sure what it is, but you must have an operation," the doctor had warned. A hospital! Anna had never been in a hospital, even to visit. So far from home. How would her family survive? Besides, people only went to a hospital to die. She could think of no one who had entered one and returned home, but finally, as she knew she would, she submitted and plans were made. The children would stay at the home of brother John for a few days. Even though they loved their Uncle John and their cousins, Anna knew homesickness would overcome them. So arrangements were made for a widowed neighbor lady to come stay with the children after their visit with John, and she would tend to them until Anna was home and quite able to resume her role as wife and mother.

Telling her children goodbye was the very worst part. Although upset, the boys were anxious to have a visit at their cousins' home. The two youngest were not fully able to comprehend the problem, but Emma, between sobs, moaned that Momma was sure to die. As in any trial or sickness, Emma grieved that someone 'was sure to die.'

"Emma, my little worrier. Momma will be home soon. You must now be the Momma in my place." With this, she quickly turned and motioned to Fred. Thus they started the long drive to the city. Anna, on the road, looked back at her beloved homestead and prayed, "Please let me return."

Many times in her long life Anna would relive the moments she awoke after the operation. Intense pain seared her body, and a blackness kept pushing her back into a deep pit. The stench of ether permeated the surroundings, and as her sluggish eyes opened, through a yellow haze of pain and misery, she was aware of dark forms surrounding the bed, kneeling, heads bent. *I'm in heaven. I died and went to heaven. Angels are all around me.* Then sleep came once more.

Someone was calling her name. Disturbing her. Patting her face. "You must wake up now." Anna looked into the face of one who had knelt by her bed.

"Are you an angel?"

"No, not quite," smiled the young woman. "We are nuns, and we have been praying for you for a long time."

Nuns! Anna had never seen a nun before. But feeling too poorly to be embarrassed, she whispered "Thank you."

And the days that followed were wretched.

The thirst was overwhelming, but she could have no liquids. When she slept, she dreamed of her well, with the cold water waiting to be dipped. It lapped in waves, beckoning. As the nurse washed her face, her feverish dry lips would try to draw moisture from the wash cloth. *I'll surely starve to death, or die of thirst!*

After several days, when the nurses helped her from the bed, on rubbery legs and bent with pain, Anna took her first steps. When the doctor was comfortable there would be no infection, as was often the case, he asked the long awaited question. "Anna, how would you like to go home tomorrow?" "Yes, yes!" Home. How good that sounded. They would get news to Fred and he would come for her tomorrow. When they left the hospital the next day, Anna did not look back. She wanted to leave the memories of pain behind. Finally, on the long uncomfortable ride, her home came into view. The prayer had been answered. She had returned.

Anna lay her head back in the chair. That was so many years ago. She remembered the joy of her children when she had arrived home, and the hot summer, and all the work and chores that went with it. She had vowed, during her time of deprivation of water at the hospital, to drink from her well— to drink and drink the fresh cold water, to never take it for granted again. Strangely though, as things got back to normal, she had forgotten her terrible thirst, forgotten until now.

Her strength had been slow to return and she was impatient with herself. Emma had been a summer baby, and Anna felt the same frustration she had felt then—wanting, needing to be strong, but unable to. At summer's end, however, she was regaining her strength and was able to do more each day. It had been difficult, keeping up with the unending chores, and tending to her family. Probably the hardest part was not being able to lift anything. Carrying buckets of water, hauling wood for the stove, hoisting a child to her hip were a natural part of life. Now she thought how differently it would have been to have had the conveniences that were available today.

19

Probably the most profound change in Anna's life had come with the arrival of electricity. When had it been? What a delightful experience to go to town and see the stores lighted! Only a few homes had the advantage. Finally the big day came—a Delco battery system was installed in the basement of their home. As she remembered, there were ten or twelve glass boxes. Fred would start a motor that gave the precious current that provided the lights in their home. They were one of very few families to enjoy such a luxury. It had been wonderful when neighbors and friends came calling to see the amazing invention called electric lights, but it was used sparingly, for only short periods of time.

The thrill, the absolute thrill, came to pass in the summer of '26. Fred and Anna had seen airplanes in the sky. Few, very few. The sound of an airplane approaching would bring a body outside to gawk upwards no matter what one was doing. Amazing! How did they do this? The first to fly over brought a fear to them. Anna herself had a nervous feeling until the contraption was out of sight. Who would be crazy enough to fly through the air? Anna and her husband shook their heads, happy to know their feet were firmly on the ground. Never, no, never, would they long to fly in a thing that looked so tiny in the sky but was large enough to carry a man high above them.

Yet one day Anna had seen Fred across the field stop the team and plow. He gazed at the sky for a long time. He confided in her that night. "How fine it would be to have a bird's eye view of the earth. To follow the farms and see my brother and other neighbors in their fields, watching, waving. What does it look like? To fly so high? To view our beloved river from overhead—following it like a silver ribbon."

"And would you go up if you ever had the chance?"

"No", Fred replied. "No, I think I'll stay put right where the good Lord intended me."

The newspaper that was delivered to the farm told of a man who was planning a sensational feat. His name was Lindbergh, and they called him Lindy for short. He was to carry the mail from St. Louis to Chicago and back again. What a conquest that would be! Even more exciting was the fact that the flight would stop at Peoria, a big city close by, go straight over little South Pekin, then fly west of their own small town. This route gave a distinct chance that they would be able to see the plane carrying the brave young pioneer above the prairie.

Then one evening at dark, they heard it. The plane! Running outside, the family heard the motor's whine long before a tiny light was visible. It seemed so strange. A moving light in the sky. Had the neighbors seen? It had gone right over their farm! The next day in town, yes, Fred had talked to several who had heard the plane motor break the stark quiet of the country side.

"But right over your farm, Fred! If it were daylight, you

could wave."

And then came an idea. Fred mulled it over in his mind for several days. Dare he? Every night at almost exactly the same time the tiny light dotted the sky, and one evening he whispered to Anna. Gathering the family around the light pole in the barn yard he waited for the hum in the distance. As the light came into view, Fred pushed the pole light switch off and on, off and on. They waited. Then, as if in answer, the light in the sky blinked off and on, off and on.

There had been much elation. He had seen their light. He had returned their signal! Such excitement. Even the dog shared in the merriment, barking, and running in circles, though he knew not why. After calming and bedding everyone, Anna and Fred lay in their bed and stared at the dark ceiling, reveling in the glory that was theirs.

"We did it Anna! We did it. Can you believe? Lindy saw us! And he actually signaled back. Such an important man. But maybe he feels very alone up there, and our little light is a friendly beacon in the vast darkness below. We'll try again tomorrow night."

And they did. Again two lights flashed to one another in a gesture of friendliness and respect. So, for more times than Anna could remember, someone would announce, "Here comes Lindy!" And a camaraderie was born between a farm family and a young man soaring the skies. In the years to come, the young man no longer flew over the farm, but went on to other quests, gained fame, knew tragedy. The family rejoiced with him, grieved with him and missed him. Yet whenever one stood close to the light pole in the barnyard at evening, the sweet sound of "Here comes Lindy!" would echo in the stillness. Looking up, there would be an empty sky, save for an occasional twinkling star.

Could that have been over 50 years ago? Am I really turning 96 at the end of August?

'Why do we always live for tomorrow when we are young? We want to grow older, get our families raised, be out of debt. And if you're lucky, you make it. But what then? Then, we want to go back. The irony! Those were the best times in my life. I just didn't know it then.'

Anna as a young lady.

**Anna and Fred on their wedding day.
December 24, 1902**

George, Albert and Emma Volk

Elsie
(Little Elly)

Fred and Anna at their home near Green Valley

Fred and Anna's home after it had been remodeled.

Anna at 94 years of age.

Johann Phillip Weyhrich

20

Anna mused back to her childhood. She and Momma were pitting cherries. So many dishpans full of the juicy ripe beauties. So many jars to fill, but Poppa loved cherry pie, so it was tinged with a labor of love. The sun was getting hot on the little side porch where they sat. Anna had pushed up her long sleeves, and juice was running down her arms and dripping from her elbows. Glancing up, Anna noticed a man walking toward them down the long, sandy lane.

"Momma?"

Momma shifted uneasily, but did not arise. From under the shade tree, the sleeping dog lifted his head, and the hair on his neck bristled. A soft growl left his throat.

"Stay!" Momma commanded.

The dog grew silent but remained alert. The stranger approached the porch. He was disheveled and acted peculiarly. Keeping a keen eye on the dog, the man started making gestures with his hands, pointing to his ears and mouth and shaking his head 'no'.

Momma gave him a cynical look. "He's telling us he cannot hear or speak."

The stranger then made more gestures to indicate he was hungry, needed food.

"Anna, go inside and bring out bread. Put some butter on it."

Anna hurried, not wanting to leave Momma outside alone. She returned, placing the bread on the table and motioned him to come get it. Picking up the bread, he turned to leave. Acting on impulse, for reasons she never did know, Anna picked up one of the empty dish pans and with a wooden spoon started beating it wildly. The clamor startled the deceiver and he proclaimed a loud "No!" Running through the yard, he beat a hasty retreat down the lane, all the while shouting his objections. Anna ran after him, beating the dishpan, her long skirt swirling dust and her long braids bouncing on her shoulders.

Momma watched in breathless amazement, her hands clasping the sides of her face. Her daughter finally turned and slowly ran back to her on the porch, a look of triumph on her face.

"Anna! How...what were you thinking?" Momma sputtered.

"I don't know. It all happened so fast. I took a chance, and I was right."

The pair looked at one another, and Momma shook her head and laughed. Anna did too. The tension melted as mother and daughter laughed till tears rolled. Momma got a towel and poured a dipper of water from the bucket nearby. She wiped her little girl's grimy, sweaty face, then looked deeply into the blue eyes.

This impulsive child. This little one so different from the others. Does she know no fear? She is not meek or reserved like most children her age. A good girl, but...and Momma thought hard...spirited. Yes, that was the word. Spirited. And that, as she had known all along, was what made her so special to Poppa.

"Momma, shall we tell Poppa?"

Momma paused, thought hard. "Of course! Now let's get back to work."

Every spring thereafter, as Anna pitted cherries, alone, with her children or her grandchildren, she would recall the hot sunny morning so long ago when she and Momma had a visitor come-a-calling. She would chuckle remembering her less than gracious manners, and wondered if he had enjoyed Momma's fresh bread and butter.

Now Anna wanted to sleep in her chair. She couldn't. Why was her mind racing so? So many things were coming back to her today. Things she hadn't thought about in years. A fear wafted through her. Was she going to die?

They say your life flashes before you when you die. But that was nonsense. She was fine. Just a little pain in her stomach. Something she ate.

21

Anna's thoughts drifted back to when her own Momma had passed. She had lived for many years after Poppa had died. *How old had Momma been? Eighty. It seems like she was eighty.* She had lived with her son and his family on the home place, close enough for Anna's family to visit fairly often. When she and the children went alone, it was a very scary experience to cross the old bridge over the river. Before coaxing the mare onto the wooden boards, the children were instructed to be quiet, to not make a sound, and sit very still in their seats in the buggy. As the horse gingerly clopped her hooves across the bridge, the water swirled deeply beneath them. Anna breathed a sigh of relief each time the bridge was left behind.

Momma had always looked the same. She still wore dark colored, mostly black, long dresses and black stockings. All the older women her age seemed to dress in a similar manner with their hair pulled into a knot on the back of their heads. The last few times Anna had seen her, Momma had seemed a little more frail with each visit.

Anna couldn't remember how she got the news that her mother was very low, but she did remember running and fetching Fred and driving in their car as fast as a car could go in those days. Anna wanted to be there now! Why was the car so slow? She felt that if she got out and ran, she would arrive sooner. Finally the lane appeared before them, and Fred worked the floor shift to gain momentum for the car to travel through the deep sand. Half way up, the wheels started spinning, the motor groaned, and Fred announced that they were "stuck deep." Hearing that, Anna flung open the door and ran for the house. It was difficult trudging in the sand and she felt, as in a bad dream, as though she were being forced back. Her heart was pounding and she prayed to get there in time to see Momma and tell her good bye.

Her brother had seen them arrive and was holding the door open. "How is she? Am I in time?" she queried between gasps for breath.

"She's very poor. I'm glad you are here." Anna followed him. Her legs felt weak and her hands ice cold. The bedroom was dark because the shades were pulled. It was difficult to adjust her vision after the bright sunlight outside.

There is death in this room. A chill caused her to tremble. Momma looked small and frail in her bed. Anna took her thin, limp hand and held it in both of hers. Momma didn't move. Her brother's wife was crying, but Anna didn't. She had prepared for this for a long time. It wasn't a shock as when Poppa died. Now that Anna was here with her mother, she felt more self control.

Momma's breathing was shallow, barely noticeable, and then it stopped. Without a gasp or a sigh, her soul left her body. Anna could not move. She only sat and looked at Momma, and still held her hand. The once strong and domineering woman who Anna had obeyed and feared, but laughed with and loved, was gone.

Anna thought of the hollyhocks in her own garden, strong

and straight. When bent by heavy winds, they would again
arise to weather the elements, and be made even stronger.
But in the autumn of their life, the delicate blooms would
slowly droop as a tired head bowed down. The leaves would
then wither and come together as folded hands. The stems
would bend, not unlike a worn old body, until the row of
once colorful, brazen beauties were old and tired, ready for
the harsh winter that would claim them.

Then someone removed Momma's hand from hers and
pulled the white sheet over the lifeless face. *And that, is that.
All these years of thinking about it, and it's here. It's happened.*

The minister came, others arrived. There were tears and
sobs, prayers and planning. Just as when Poppa had died
Anna had a great need to be alone.

"Take me home," she gasped to Fred. "I'll come back
later."

Wordlessly they drove home. Suddenly Anna knew the
feeling of having no parents, and it seemed strange, hollow.
Even though Momma was old, there was still a sense of
security, stability. Now both were gone. Already she felt
older. 'Now I'm the last generation,' she thought. After
relating the news to her children, she went to her room and
slept, and dreamed dreams of long ago and happier times.

Two days later, as Momma lay in the side room, the
people came—relatives, neighbors, friends, young and old,
some in autos, some in horse and buggy. They were tearful
yet consoling, bearing food and flowers. Men removed their
hats and nodded uncomfortably. Women soaked their
hankies as they gazed upon Momma for the last time.
Children, bathed, hair sleeked and dressed in their Sunday
best, appeared wide eyed, curious, and more than a little
frightened as they filed quietly into the room. For most, this

would be the first time to see a dead person. Adhering to the stern warning given before leaving home, none spoke or were spoken to. The stiffness was relaxed only upon seeing a friend or cousin, and a shy smile or an unobtrusive little wave was exchanged.

When Anna opened her eyes early the next morning, she thought, *Something's wrong. What? Oh yes, yes, Momma. We bury her today.*

She rolled over and didn't want to get up, see anyone. She buried her face in her pillow, and all the faces from the day before passed through her mind. Some she had not seen for ages. Many had come a long distance. How nice it would have been under different circumstances. *But enough.* She must get up and fix breakfast. The mourning clothes had been laid out the night before. After chores and tidying up, the family would depart for the church. They must be seated with the relatives before others arrived.

Once again, familiar, and some unfamiliar, faces surrounded her. The minister spoke comforting words, funeral songs were sung, heads were bowed in prayer. The ladies in black veiled hats and dark conservative dresses, and the men in dark suits gave the little church a somber appearance in contrast to the bright sunlight that streamed through the windows.

At the last second, as she was to give her Mother her last goodbye, Anna was unprepared. She simply patted her hand and walked away from her. So on a lovely June day, Momma was laid to rest in the little cemetery that adjoined the church yard. She had joined Poppa. Now her name would be engraved on the huge stone that marked the eternal resting place of the two people that had given Anna life, molded her into who she was, loved her and now left her.

Anna stirred in her chair. *That's how I told Elly goodbye. I patted her hand.* Elly. She could still see the lovely blue dress she had tearfully chosen for her daughter's burial. On it, Anna had pinned a small golden double heart engraved with the names of Elly and her niece, the niece that she had loved. It was her only prized piece of jewelry. She remembered Elly's pride when told that her 'Oifey', as she had nicknamed her, had been given money to buy herself a treat at the fair. Instead she had chosen the pin. Elly treasured it and wore it often. So it had seemed only natural to bury it with her. Now Anna's child, her parents, her husband, brothers and sisters, and all before her were gone, waiting for her. Anna had the uneasy feeling it would not be long.

22

There were so many colorful characters back then. Anna remembered that many people had nicknames, now she seldom heard one. She had known a Shorty, a Fatty, a Red, a Cutie, a Boo, a Windy, a Skinny, but she was glad that nicknames were on the way out. People should be called by the names their parents gave them, not some silly name that described them.

One character Anna certainly remembered was from a time when she, Fred, and the girls had been visiting Momma. Returning home, it was getting dark and Fred was driving his Ford cautiously. He hadn't owned a car very long and didn't drive much at night. It was a hot, dry evening and dust surrounded the car as it approached the Mackinaw River bridge. Squinting into the distance, Fred slowed even more. Something was ahead, something bright, some sort of lights.

"Look there! What is that Anna?"

Anna saw the brightness. It was just on the other side of the bridge.

"I don't know. Turn around!"

"No," Fred replied. We've got to get home. Let's see

what's going on."

From the back seat, the girls' eyes shone with excitement. "Down!" Anna commanded. "Get to the floor."

Then fear overtook excitement as Fred slowly moved ahead. No one spoke as the girls huddled together on the back seat floor. Elly started to cry, and Emma cradled her tightly.

"It looks like lamps," said Fred. "Lots of lamps. Who would be so crazy to be burning lamps here?"

Crossing the bridge now, they could see several kerosene lamps strung up through the trees, giving off an eerie glow. Suddenly a man appeared, waving his arms.

"Don't stop!" Anna cried.

More out of curiosity than anything, Fred stopped and cranked the window ever so slightly.

"Soda, I have soda to sell," yelled the man. Sure enough, he held up several bottles of soda drink. Upon hearing this, the girls made a speedy transition from cowering to fearlessness.

"Poppa, please. May we have a soda drink?"

"Let's get out of here!" Anna cried. "The man is crazy!" Someone could be hiding here with him. It's too lonely and dark to stop."

Apparently Fred agreed, because he quickly cranked up the window and tromped on the gas pedal.

"Who would be down here at this time of night selling something?" Anna exclaimed. "No one hardly ever travels this road. All the lanterns. He went to so much work. He must be mad. I can't believe it!" Anna rambled. "A man at the river with a tub of drinks to sell."

But Fred only shook his head in bewilderment, and the girls knelt on the seat looking out the back as the glow from the flickering lights faded in the distance.

They never found out who the man was. It seemed no one they knew had traveled the road that night. Was he a person trying to set up a business in an impractical spot, or someone with an evil motive? They had talked about it often, but everyone felt sure they had done the right thing by not stopping. Still, Anna would always wonder, *Who was the strange character at the side of the road those many years ago? Should we have stopped? No, of course not!*

23

An October morn came to mind. Anna had never seen a bluer sky, a typical Indian Summer day to be sure. Crisp clean air. She wished to be out of doors all day. Even though all the children, except Elly, were gone and had families of their own, her days were still full. The farm and her home seemed like a huge ship to be maneuvered. Someone must always be there to guide and to protect, to keep things on course, and complete the multitude of duties that kept things running smoothly around the clock.

This was corn picking time, but so unlike the days when the men would wearily walk along side a wagon and pick and husk the ears by hand. Now a tractor and corn picker were in the field, looking and sounding foreign, but admittedly making harvest time much easier. A team and wagon were still used to haul the picked corn to the cribs. Anna couldn't bear the thought of no horses, of everything being mechanical. It still, after all these many years, gave her a pleasant feeling to behold a sight such as the one she now witnessed. The wagon was laden with golden ears, and the team of horses easily and slowly pulled their burden across the fields.

Her son George and his family lived on the next farm and he and Fred worked together to blend the two farms as one. Anna reluctantly went into the house, little suspecting the fearsome tragedy that would soon occur, almost leaving her a widow, and causing bodily harm to Fred that would stay with him all his days.

Things were going well. It was not hot, and a gentle breeze was stirring the dried corn stalks. The skeletal stalks that were picked looked barren next to the ones still laden with their golden yield. Fred would continue to run the machine while his son returned to his farm to empty the wagon. But then it seemed something was not running smoothly, perhaps clogged up. Circling the picker, Fred removed his straw hat and wiped his face and silvery hair with his blue handkerchief. Stuffing it back into his hip pocket, he replaced the straw hat to shield his eyes from the sun. There was the trouble! Corn stalks had wrapped around the shucking rollers of the corn picker. He reached down to loosen the stalks. Suddenly, with a great jolt, he was pulled into the drive wheel. It had caught his coat sleeve, the sleeve of his new overall jacket. His first and only instinct was to pull back, to pull and pull. 'I'm caught, I'm caught!' he thought frantically. He couldn't holler, couldn't cry for help. Self survival instinctively set in. He miraculously reached into his pants pocket and retrieved a pocket knife. Not remembering later how he did it, he opened the knife blade and tried in vain to cut his clothing. Searing pain drove through Fred's shoulder, and he felt a great tearing, but still he pulled away. What seemed like forever was only a short time, while he was held prisoner by this wretched contraption.

Even while Fred knew his strength could not withstand much longer, his son was unhurriedly driving the empty wagon back to the field where his father was in great distress. Holding the reins in one hand and shielding his eyes with the other, he scanned the field and surveyed the acreage still to be picked—probably half through. *That's strange.* There was no movement from the machinery. It seemed to be standing still. When he saw great billows of black smoke pouring from the tractor, he slapped the reins across the horses' broad rumps and hollered. With dangerous speed the wagon bounced across the field. Without coming to a full stop, George jumped off the wagon and beheld the awful sight that he feared would greet him.

Fred had managed to resist—to pit man's strength against machine. His son's first reaction was to go to his father and try to pull him out.

"Turn it off! Off!" Fred gasped. Before George could turn it off, the tractor sputtered and was quiet. Pulling out of his shredded clothing, Fred dropped to the ground, trembling, and so weak he could scarcely move.

"Dad, oh Dad!" his ashen faced son cried. "Are you hurt bad? What happened?" He helped his father to his feet and gingerly placed him in the wagon and drove him across the rough fields to the house.

Anna was under the big tree making lye soap for the long winter. Always keeping a close watch on the fields, she had seen the team and wagon appear as a tiny dot, and as it grew larger and closer, she stopped her work and peered from under her broad straw hat. *Dinner time? So soon? No.* She had been working hard, but time never got completely away from her. Something was wrong. She could only see a driver. She stood fast, fear gnawing at her. In the wagon, spent and dazed, Fred moaned, "Don't scare your mother. Tell her I'm OK."

But when Anna saw Fred, she knew he was not OK. "What happened? Fred!"

"I got caught in the picker. But don't worry, I'll be alright."

Elly had raced out of the kitchen, screaming, "Poppa, Momma, what has happened?"

George had carefully helped his father get out of the wagon and guided him to sit on the side of the nearby horse tank. Hurriedly, he raced to the shed to bring Fred's automobile to the threesome and ordered, "Momma, Elly, get Dad into the back seat."

It had been horrendous, trying to get the injured man into the car, and trying to make him comfortable. Elly had run back into the house and brought pillows to be placed around her pale and suffering father. Finally, with Anna and Fred in the back seat, brother and sister in front, the car sped away from the farm. Thus began the long trek to the doctor's office in the city.

Following the painful journey, Fred was escorted into the doctor's office by the concerned trio. After a lengthy examination, the doctor determined no bones were broken, but he had incurred a dislocated shoulder along with bruises and abrasions. All Fred could mutter was "I'm not going to the hospital."

As the entire story had been revealed to the doctor, he listened intently and was astounded by what he heard. As he wrapped, strapped, and mended the injured body before him, he could only imagine the terrible misfortune that he could be tending to if things had gone differently.

"Fred, Fred. You are truly a remarkable man. Anyone with lesser strength—well, we won't even think about it. And the fact that you had on a brand new jacket certainly helped. But I've never, in all my years of practice heard of such a thing. Having the presence of mind to find your knife, open it, and try to cut yourself out. Unbelievable! And then to burn out the tractor!" And he shook his head as he boxed pain pills, for he knew the pain was and would be fearsome.

So Fred had returned home to family and neighbors, both humbled and somewhat embarrassed, but very much thankful to God to be alive. The hardest part for Anna was the fact that Fred never entirely regained the strength in his arm. For years after, he squeezed the red rubber ball as the doctor ordered, to strengthen and maintain. Never once did he complain, and never, after his doctor's release, did it deter him from performing his chores and duties. And it broke her heart to know of his inner turmoil, of not being what he once was, that a small part of his strength and independence had been taken away, but it mattered not to Anna. He was alive and with her.

They rarely talked about it, but more times than she could remember, that fateful October morn that had started so beautifully and ended so ugly, came back to remind her how vulnerable humans can be. In a swift second, her life and family could have been changed forever.

24

But that was long ago. Everything Anna remembered was long ago. She thought of the time on the farm when she was a young mother...*It seems I had two children. No, three. I had Emma. She was a toddler. I was hanging out my wash on the line. The boys were playing in the dirt with spoons. Emma was playing with the clothes pins. Fred was somewhere by the barn.* It became very clear now. She could almost feel the breeze as she hung the sweet, soapy smelling sheets on the clothesline. Emma began darting in and out under the clothes and playing peek-a-boo. Anna laughed as a gust suddenly whipped the sheet and caused her surprised baby to plop on her bottom.

It seemed to be getting dark. *Funny. Not a cloud in the sky. It had been so bright and sunny a short time ago.* Hoping it didn't rain, she continued her task, but an eerie feeling set in. It unsettled her. All around it seemed to be darker, but it was morning! Was there a problem with her eyes? She felt a gentle tugging on her skirt.

"Momma, is it night time already?" her son queried.

"No, no, now go play with your brother." *So it was getting dark!* She felt fearful.

"Stay with your sister," she told her sons.

She hastened towards the dinner bell to beckon Fred, but he too was puzzled, and was already coming hurriedly across the barn yard.

"What is it?" Anna shouted. "What's happening?"

"I don't know," Fred replied. They gathered the children and stood on the porch as it grew darker.

"Look Fred! The chickens are going to roost!"

Emma had fallen asleep on her mother's shoulder. The boys, sensing something was wrong, stayed close to their parents. "Lord help us. It must be the end of the world!" Anna cried. She had been so afraid. She'd not meant to frighten her sons, but now they were wailing because Momma was upset. When the darkness had peaked, a horse and buggy pulled into the barnyard. It was their neighbor Andrew. He was on his way home, he explained, when the darkness set in.

"What is it?" Fred asked. "Look, the chickens are even roosting."

"I don't know for sure," replied Andrew. "But my father told me about something like this that happened in the old country. I was just a lad and don't remember, but he said it didn't last long and the sun came out again. I'd forgotten all about it." And as Andrew's horse slept nearby, the group stood and watched and waited.

Growing weary from holding the sleeping child, Anna urged all to go into the house.

"No, I must get home to my family. Mary is probably worried sick."

Bidding Andrew be careful, Anna and the children went inside. After placing the sleeping baby in her bed, and giving the boys a cup of milk, she rejoined Fred on the porch.

"It seems to be getting lighter," he proclaimed.

Yes, yes, it was brighter. Slowly, slowly, the day grew lighter and clearer. The fear was gone, but not the mystery.

Later they had learned of something called an eclipse. Anna did not understand, but thought, *I'll surely have something to tell my grandchildren!* And she had! And they never tired of hearing about the morning that turned into night!

25

Another moment on the farm had returned to her thoughts many times. The children, with the exception of Elly, had all married and left home, but the routine remained unchanged. The big horses were still very much prized possessions. Fred took great care to lock all gates and stalls each evening. Fences were carefully mended during the months that he was not busy in the fields. But, whether due to human error or the craftiness of the animal, an escape took place that caused a commotion, the likes of which had never been seen by family or neighbor.

All had been quiet that April night. It was two o'clock in the morning and the three family members slumbered heavily after a strenuous days work. Anna was the first to hear it, a thumping sound, metal clanging. *The wind? No. There was a distant cry. An animal sound.* Shaking Fred awake, eyes wide in the dark, she whispered, "What could it be?" They listened.

Now Fred was pulling on his clothes, hurrying, bumping into things.

"Get a light. I have no idea what it is, but something is in trouble."

A frightened Elly emerged from her room, for she, too, had heard the unidentifiable noise, and was prepared to go with her father to find the source.

Anna waited in the doorway. The chilly night air caused her to pull her wrap closely around her. "Please be careful," she called to the pair as they headed towards the commotion. Within a moment, Elly and Fred ran back to her, looking shocked and sickened.

"The mare, she's fallen into the cesspool. She's in head first, past her front legs."

Anna clutched her chest. The pool had always been a worry to her. Covered with only a tin sheet and several boards, the children had always been warned, and had obediently stayed away. Now, however, an unsuspecting animal had apparently wandered astray and was in a life-threatening situation.

Hurriedly, Fred turned the crank on the big wall phone— a continuous ring to alert the neighbors. One by one, they were roused from their slumbers, knowing that news of an emergency would be revealed on the line.

If a bird had been soaring high above that night, it would have seen farm house lights sporadically blink on below. Soon car lights left driveways and headed down the dirt roads leading to the Volk farm, where a neighbor was in need.

Someone, Fred never learned who, had notified the fire department in the village. But before they arrived, a dozen or so men had figured, assessed, calculated, and speculated the best strategies to execute a rescue. All ideas were futile, but then the fire truck pulled in. It was not a common sight to see a fire or fire truck in the country in the early 1930s. The farmers felt admiration for the handful of men that climbed down, but still felt a wave of resentment. They were used to handling their own problems. They liked their independence and didn't care for outside interference, but the brigade had pulleys and belts and equipment needed to rescue a suffering beast. Lanterns were hung in tree limbs, car lights were alternately shone on the rescuers so as not to run down batteries. Anna had two big granite coffee pots perking, and was still barely able to keep the men's cups full.

With much shouting and clamor, the animal was raised into the air and gently guided to the ground. It lay weak and frightened, but apparently and surprisingly unharmed.

When finally Fred slowly led the horse into the barn, both city and country gentlemen shook hands and expressed thanks to one another. As the cars left, carrying tired, yet exhilarated passengers, the eastern sky was bathed in a peach hue, proclaiming a new morning....a new day. A time to be home, where livestock waited, and wives and children were anxious.

26

Anna thought the year was 1915. Sometime around there. It was hard to remember. The house was small for three girls and two boys. Something must be done. She and Fred had talked halfheartedly for sometime about adding on rooms, but now the time had come. Fred had contacted Mr. Hilling, a builder from Manito, and the plans were started. Fred would do much of the work himself. He would make the cement blocks for the foundation and a new coal bin, using gravel from the big gravel pit that covered the northeast section of the farm. The gravel pit had been an unexpected resource on the property.

It had always fascinated Fred, this deposit that was left here so many years ago. He had once read that gravel was deposited during the Glacial period, and could be hundreds of feet above present rivers. He knew that was so, because when he stood atop the bluff above the pit, he could see his beloved Mackinaw river. But it was beyond his thinking how long ago that would have been, and how his farm and the surrounding prairie must have looked. Now this precious material from the earth would be used to form concrete and mortar to lay the foundation and give support to the home he was expanding for his growing family.

So the work began. The children delighted in watching and helping their father make the cement blocks. After much gravel had been hauled, the mixer, which was powered by a gas engine, was utilized. It held five scoops of gravel and three scoops of cement, then sand and water were added. The mixture was poured into forms and left to set overnight to dry. When the blocks had set, they were removed and the process was repeated over and over again.

One day, Frieda, the second oldest daughter, had been playing in the sand. Anna could remember well the excitement when Frieda's hand scooped up a dime and a nickel—no matter to her where it had come from or who could have lost it. The shiny coins were hers to do with as she pleased. For sure, every new load of sand brought in was thoroughly sifted by the small fingers of the three girls, hoping to find more hidden treasure.

For weeks, Mr. Hilling worked, adding to the upstairs and building closets. When the roof was partially removed for the addition, Emma, Frieda, and Elly spent nights at Annie Ripper's home. How excited they were, to stay the night at their Momma's nieces' home, then to go back to the flurry of activity, of seeing their house changing so every day. By the time the work was completed, three bedrooms had been added, also three closets upstairs. Anna would now enjoy her new pantry, enlarged kitchen, back porch, and a big wonderful front porch, where her family could rest or play.

The house was finished with stucco, which was very popular then. A man by the name of Fred Shores from Pekin did this job, and Fred and Anna were pleased with his expertise. When Mr. Hilling had completed the carpentry work, and the rooms were ready, Mr. Harry Neese from Green Valley came to hang the wallpaper. The family had spent hours around the kitchen table looking at wallpaper books, so many beautiful samples! Bright, curly flowers, subdued stripes and shapes. How could one decide? If only they could see the completed work. After much debate, disagreement, and reasoning, Anna had the final say. There was some disappointment, but it had been fun, and everyone had been a little bit relieved when the final decisions were made. It had looked lovely. The smell of paste and new paper filled the house, and when Mr. Sanders, also from Pekin, painted the house trim white and gray, the tremendous chore was proclaimed finished. The family was proud of their new home, content and grateful, and they gave thanks.

THE END OF AUGUST

27

Another winter passed, and with spring, the roads were very muddy. Fred and the boys hauled gravel from the pit. They would remove the wagon box from the running gears of the farm wagon, and place several two-by-six planks for the floor. They would then hitch the team and drive back to the gravel pit, load gravel on the planks, and walk the great distance back to the main road. Driving down the very middle of the muddy road and lifting the two middle planks, the gravel was spread. The next two planks were then lifted and so on until the wagon was empty. They worked all day long, day after day, until the road was covered to the neighbors' property on either side. When completed, the team was hitched to a drag that would smooth and level. How tiring it had been for them! All the loading and unloading was by hand. Others also came with teams and wagons to haul gravel and to connect with the place where their bordering neighbors' roads had ended. For years to come, the Sand Prairie Township would dig many loads to gravel the surrounding roads.

In later years, when the telephone was introduced, after the road work was completed, the neighbor men would

117

gather and follow the telephone wires and repair what was faulty. Phones had made a tremendous difference in their rural life. They had connected families with one another in a way never expected, so it was vital that the lines were maintained. Everyone had a different ring. Anna could remember hers. It was one long and three shorts. Of course if she heard the phone ringing ten or fifteen short rings she knew it was an emergency—her help was needed.

When someone passed away, Anna recalled, the dreaded short rings were a summons for the men to come and help dig the grave. Of all emergencies, this was the one Fred disliked the most. It meant the loss of a friend or relative. In winter it was nigh impossible to dig the dirt, but with picks and shovels they would labor till the task was completed. It could not be postponed. Whether a blizzard raged or ice covered the ground, somehow the men managed.

Yes, the telephone had been a blessing, an instrument used to come to their neighbor's aid.

Again Fred and the boys had repaired harness all winter, and now, another planting was about to happen. He would pick out the best corn from the corn crib. Fred never bought seed corn. Farmers were very self sufficient. With this, Anna would start to save her best, large hen eggs until she had enough to place under ten or more hens. Each hen had at least ten to fifteen eggs in its nest. She always made sure her hands were very clean to gather the eggs because if one's hands were greasy, she'd been told the eggs wouldn't hatch.

The patient mother hens would sit on their nests day and night, only leaving to eat and drink. In addition to this, Anna would fill an incubator which held close to two hundred eggs. She could remember the box-like thing had kerosene lamps to warm the eggs.

For the brooder hens, whose eggs did not hatch, Anna would take baby chicks from the incubator and tuck them under the unsuspecting hens. The hen would raise them as her own and she would dote on the new brood that would eventually grow to provide the family with fresh eggs or delicious fried chicken for Sunday dinners.

28

An unfortunate episode had occurred early one winter. *George must have been around twelve.* It had been a very cold morning. As the sun rose higher in the sky, so had the temperature risen, enough to cause trickles of water to worm their way from the banks of snow standing in the barn lot. The boys had been restless and eager to be outside. A rollicking snow ball fight had left them breathless, and their clothes were crusty with white spots, denoting the accuracy of the slushy weapons hurled by brother against brother.

Seeking a more adventurous romp, George decided it was time to let Trotsie, his pony, out of her winter confines. Perhaps, if Momma allowed, he would bridle her and ride down the road.

"Nonsense! It's too cold. Wait till spring."

"But Momma, it's nice out, really," George had insisted. "And Trotsie needs some exercise. And didn't I hear you say this morning you needed coffee? I could ride to the store for you and save Poppa the trip."

True, she hated to see Fred make a trip to town for one item. It was better to wait till her list grew. But still, she needed coffee for breakfast to serve with the streusel she was now popping into the oven.

"Get ready, I'll meet you at the gate with the money."

Not quite believing what he had heard, George said "Yes, Momma," and headed towards the barn before she could change her mind.

Trotsie was ready to feel the weight of someone on her back, to snort the cold stinging air, to gallop, or trot, whatever the rider willed. At the gate, Anna watched her son place the coin in his pocket, and after much warning and cautioning, George left the driveway feeling much older than he had an hour ago, overwhelmed with a sense of responsibility and independence. His first trip to the village alone!

Riding high in the saddle, George suppressed the desire to heel the pony in the flank and let her run as fast as she could. He could feel Trotsie straining at the reins, urging, glad to be free of the enclosure that had held her captive for the past months, but the roads were not clear. The chuck holes were full of ice and one slip of a small hoof could be tragic.

On either side, high snow drifts lined the narrow road leading to town, sparkling from the bright sun. An illusion of a long mysterious tunnel was rendered to George, and it seemed to narrow into infinity. He passed Andrew's place, the only farm on the way, but saw no one. No one to wave to, to show off for. He had envisioned Andrew telling Mary as they sat at dinner, that the Volk boy was surely growing up, that he had seen him a awhile ago alone, on his pony, riding towards town. And Mary would surely exclaim that it didn't seem possible that Anna's boys were old enough to be doing such a thing. No matter, he thought, there would be folks in town to see him.

His eyes started to tear from the cold and brightness, but he soon approached the wooden bridge that crossed over the main road that led to Pekin. Carefully, carefully, the pony stepped across the icy planks, and then the village came into view. The road curved to the right and the pair pushed on. Here it was! Green Valley! Small, safe, serene. Not many people were out—it was close to noon. Some shopkeepers went home for their dinner, but the grocery store was a busy place most of the day.

But now George got a little careless, with the store such a short distance away. He slapped the reins, causing Trotsie to burst into a full gallop. Most of the frozen water puddles had softened enough to break under the weight of a passer-by or a rambunctious child's stomping to see the ice splinter and delight in the squishy sound it made. As the excited animal rounded the corner in front of the doctor's office, George was aware of a skid, and he felt himself falling to the left, still astride his mount. A twisting, violent pain shot through his leg. Trotsie, slipping and groping for a foothold, finally stood and shook her head sideways and trembled.

George lie there, awake and aware of his injury. He knew before the crowd gathered that his leg was broken, but his spirit was also broken. He had, as the saying goes, been taken down a few notches. As he was gingerly carried to the nearby doctor's office his thoughts were of Momma. She had trusted him, warned him. When would he ever get to experience such an adventure again? He fought tears of pain and anger.

A few days later, on a cold, dreary Sunday afternoon, George lay in a makeshift bedroom downstairs. A sudden knock on the door brought Anna to her feet. There stood her brother George and his wife, cold and anxious to enter the warm room. After greetings were exchanged, Brother George removed a table cloth from a large cylinder. Lo and behold! A freezer of homemade ice cream. In the winter! The other children climbed onto the kitchen chairs to watch as Uncle pulled out the paddle and ordered Anna to bring the bowls. She scooped mounds of the wonderful treat, chock full of strawberries that had been canned in the heat of the previous summer. Uncle carried the largest bowl to his namesake, sternly admonishing him for his carelessness, but then tosseling his hair and saying, "Eat your ice cream before it melts."

29

Anna yearned to have Poppa near, to hear his stories. Even though the winters had been brutal, nothing had pleased her more than to sit at Poppa's feet, wrapped in a quilt made by Momma, and listen as he held her spellbound, telling of the things he had seen and heard. The busy summers did not afford such pleasure, but on an icy winter night, with supper done, the few hours before bedtime were monotonous. With a little begging, Poppa would commence to tell a tale to the wide-eyed Anna and her siblings as Momma sat nearby with her sewing in her lap acting uninterested, but cocking her head so as not to miss a word. This was a story he told:

It was the summer of 1869. Poppa had his own farm then, and needed a piece that had broken from his plow. He would ride to the village and wait while the blacksmith made the repairs. Upon arrival, however, he learned that the smithy was laid up with back problems.

"But I needed it right away. I had much to do at home. Someone suggested I try the shop at Circleville, a small town that lie to the northeast. I had only been there a couple of times, but the day wasn't too hot for July, so I forged ahead. Well, when I reached the town there was great excitement.

The streets were full of people, town folks and farmers from nearby.

The small hotel that stood on the main street served food and drink, and I was awful thirsty. I sat at a table and asked a gentleman next to me what was going on. He explained that the previous day the Berry Brothers, led by Brother Bill, had been parading the streets. Now, I had heard of the infamous Berry Brothers. They were descended from upright citizens who had settled on the Illinois prairie, but something went wrong with the brothers.

Everyone knew they were horse thieves. Many horses were stolen from all over the county and word has it they were kept right there close to Circleville until they could be sold. A year earlier Bill, the leader, had killed a man from Delavan, and had seriously wounded another. But somehow he had a lawyer collect the signatures of several influential men in Tazewell County and the governor pardoned him.

It seems that Bill was involved in many other underhanded escapades, but he was feared by most, and got away with it. I do know that at the time of his death, he owed many men from whom he had borrowed, but it seems no one had the nerve to approach him to collect. So the day before my visit, word reached Circleville that a posse was on the way from Pekin to serve a warrant against one of the brothers and another gang member. On Thursday before, Isaac Berry, also known as Ike, and a stranger named Britton had invited a Mr. Shaw to take part in a planned horse robbery. Well, Mr. Shaw talked with them and pretended to go along with the plan. Pleading another engagement that evening, as soon as his visitors left, Mr. Shaw notified authorities of the intended crime. A marshal and two other lawmen went out to lay in wait for the pair.

For reasons I do not know the robbery did not take place, but the officers decided to arrest the pair on suspicion. They found Berry and Britton at the saloon in Circleville, and followed them to Bill Berry's house. The pair was taken to Pekin and lodged in jail and this was about four o'clock on Friday morning.

Early that same morning an attorney called on Sheriff Pratt who lived at the jail, and using threats, succeeded in scaring Pratt by telling him he had no warrant for the arrest and the two were being illegally held. They were immediately released, and the pair returned to Circleville. Bill Berry arrived from his farm at about two in the afternoon. He climbed from his buggy and headed for the saloon where he met Brother Emanuel, Brother Ike, Britton, a Mr. McFarland, and a Mr. Daly, who was called The Peddler. Berry furnished the group with arms telling them that officers would be out after them, but to stand their ground. During the afternoon, Deputy Sheriff Henry Pratt, the jailer, and a deputy marshal procured a warrant and started for Circleville to arrest the men a second time.

By this time the gang was making plans while drinking. They say they were all dressed in black clothing. The Peddler was arguing with everyone about who had treated last. Apparently in a happy mood, the boys started parading the streets, back and forth, singing songs with Bill in the lead. They ended up at Bill Berry's house at about three in the afternoon. Someone said they heard shots fired. Probably just feeling frisky. Later they were seen sitting on the porch of the saloon, some were armed.

Around nine o' clock in the evening, I don't know why so late, Deputy Sheriff Henry Pratt, who was only twenty seven and who had served three years with the Illinois Army in the Civil War, reached the outskirts of Circleville. He was a brother to the sheriff. With him were a jailer, a Mr. Hinman, a city marshal, a Mr. Kessler, and a constable, W.F. Copes. They pulled their horses off the west side of the road on the north side of town and hitched them behind a barn. Then the posse walked up past a house to a yard gate. About then the justice of the peace yelled, "There go the men you want." The gentleman telling me the story said things got confusing then, but for certain Sheriff Pratt, who was in front of the posse, yelled for the men to stop and fired several shots in the air.

One of the pursued sprang over a rail fence, and as Pratt came near, shot a double barreled shot gun at him. Bystanders heard him cry, "I've been shot!" The city marshal caught him and kept him from falling. The members of the posse carried the young, wounded sheriff into a nearby house. The marshal left for Pekin right away to bring a doctor. It took close to three hours, and when they returned, Pratt was dead. The jailer, Mr. Hinman, had been wounded in the right shoulder and right eye. My friend at the next table said that after the gunfire stopped, the townspeople milled around until the posse left to take the body back to Pekin.

The gang members, except for Bill Berry, had fled, so the talk that morning, of course, centered around the events that had taken place the night before. Many of the people had not even gone to bed. I heard a person from Pekin sitting across the room, telling of how Berry and his gang had terrorized the towns people, walking the wooden side walks, expecting everyone to make way for them. I asked where Berry was now and someone said they saw him ride off earlier, heading for Pekin. This was not a smart thing to do, because word had spread around the whole county by now. Remember, the young man was not only a deputy sheriff, he was somewhat of a Civil War hero, too.

People started arriving in Pekin, especially folks from Delavan. I guess because of the murder a year ago. So this time, when Berry strutted around town, he was met with guns and thrown into jail. And all this happened while I was sitting in Circleville!

I was glad to leave the excitement and head for home. I'd see the blacksmith later. I remember feeling a little nervous and looking over my shoulder a lot. That was probably a little foolish, but, after all, there were several men in hiding all around. I came home and told Momma all about it. Remember?"

Momma nodded.

"That night sleep wouldn't come. Your Momma and I stared at the ceiling, whispering so as not to wake you children, wondering. Wondering whether the men had been caught. Wondering if Bill Berry was sleeping, what he was thinking. Feeling for his family. Had we known what was happening we would have never slept.

As we heard later, extra guards were placed around Berry's cell because of the mob outside, this being on Saturday night. At eleven o' clock, things were quiet and there was no apparent cause for concern. They say the streets were quieter than usual. This must have been the calm before the storm. Well, sometime after midnight the mob, they say there were more than one hundred people, marched on the jail. As they approached the cell, others emerged from the darkness. Prominent citizens, including the late General McCook, addressed the mob, calling for peace and order. They were peaceful for only awhile. Marching in military precision, the angry men reached the jail door and were met by Sheriff Pratt, brother of the slain Henry. They told him they wanted the jail keys, but he said he did not have them, and even if he did, would not hand the keys over. A shrill whistle blew, and in a very few minutes hundreds more approached. Sheriff Pratt was overpowered and the other guards were no defense. The outside door was made of wood and hardly detained them at all. At that point the Sheriff retreated to the stairs, and some of the rowdies caught him and searched him for the keys, but found none. They seized him by the throat and began to handle him harshly. Luckily, he was not injured, but was powerless against the mob. Finally tools were brought forward to break down the door leading to the front hall that connected with several cells. This door was iron and hung on solid limestone. It took one hour and forty minutes to break it down. Then another door of lattice work that closed the cell had to be broken, but a few blows with a sledge hammer caused the hinges to break and the door swung open. One cannot imagine the fearful thoughts that were running through Berry's mind. He was trapped like a penned animal.

There stood Berry, using the door as a barricade, making it difficult for the men to enter. Someone pushed through with a lantern, and Bill kicked it from his hand and drew a knife. I don't know where it came from, but someone said another person gave it to him for defense. A terrible fight broke out. A Delavan man named Livingston received a fearful wound from Berry's clasp knife. Berry continued to cut wildly, inflicting severe wounds upon a Pekin youth named Losier and another Delavanite named Brownlee. One of the wounded men later died.

About this time another lantern was brought in. As Berry drew his knife back to deliver another blow, the blade struck the brick wall and broke from the handle. Bill fell to his knees in search of the blade and someone yelled 'Stand up and fight like a man!' With that, Berry rose to his feet and was shot at five times. Only two found their mark, one in the head and one in the arm. It is said the wounded man continued to fight and struggle but the infuriated mob dragged him to a tree on the northeast corner of the Pekin courthouse square, and at about three in the morning they hanged him. I will tell you that Berry, through all the tragedy, never spoke a word or uttered any sound. He never pleaded for mercy or showed any fear.

Now while the hanging was going on, the marshal arrived with Robert Britton, whom they had just arrested. Upon hearing the tumult, the marshal took Britton to a stable for hiding. He then approached the crowd and told them he had Britton in charge. They say he had a terrible time convincing the mob to do no bodily harm to his prisoner. After things quieted down, Britton was taken to another place. As he passed the square, he witnessed his friend's body and was so overcome, he wept, almost fainted, and promised to turn state's evidence.

Well, the body was left hanging until after daylight when it was finally taken down by the coroner. By then Berry's wife, who, by the way, came from a respectable family, heard of her husband's horrible death. She arrived with her two children, a boy and a girl, and took the body back to Circleville. A funeral was held a couple of days later, and they buried him in a little cemetery close to Circleville. However, a marker was not placed on his grave. I think so no one would ever know where the body is.

On that Sunday, the same day of Berry's hanging, a jury was summoned to inquire into the cause of his death. After hearing testimony from several witnesses, including Sheriff Pratt and the surgeon, the jury returned a verdict that Berry came to his death by a pistol shot. It was fired by a person unknown.

The following December, a trial was held in Jacksonville, Illinois. That's quite a ways from here. They do that sometimes so the people will get a fair trial. I had a friend living there at the time, and he attended every day. I still have a couple of letters he sent me keeping me abreast of what happened."

Poppa arose from his chair and went into the bedroom, returning with two long forgotten letters. He carefully opened them and read to himself, and then aloud.

"Dr. Charlton was the man that examined Henry Pratt following his murder. He said that death came from a gunshot wound in the right breast. He had a pocket book in his right breast pocket. They think it might have been the warrant he was carrying. Then Marshal Kessler told the jury how he was close enough to Pratt to touch him when he was shot. He was the one who went to town to get the doctor. Next came Constable Copes. He said Pratt stopped at his home in July last to go with him as he had a little job to do. Arriving at Circleville, they stopped at the McCassen house about 250 yards from town. From somewhere the word came 'There they are!' Pratt hollered 'Hold on boys, I have business with you.' The three men were Matthew McFarland, Ike Berry and Emanuel Berry. He said he could see their features, that he had known the Berrys for a long time. Also that Pratt was hollering for them to halt or he would fire. Ike was around the corner of an iron fence. He put his gun on the fence and fired a shot, the one that killed Henry Pratt. Then Ike ran away.

Then Mr. W.H. Larimore, who was the Justice of the Peace, testified and concurred with everything else that had been said. Mr. Cassius Whitney, who was State's Attorney the summer before, said he had known Henry Pratt and that he also knew Bill Berry and brother Ike. He said he had seen Bill Berry on the evening of the 30th of July last. They were standing on a street corner in Pekin. Berry asked him if he had been getting a warrant for the arrest of Ike and his friend Britton. When he answered 'Yes', he replied that if he were me, he would not give it to the sheriff, as the boys had done nothing wrong, and there would surely be trouble if an officer went out there. The warrant was of course issued, and Mr. Whitney saw it last on the 31st of July in the jail.

Many other Circleville residents testified—Mr. Andrew Ditman, Samuel Miller, Joseph Miller, Mr. Joseph Barlow, and Mary Hamilton, who had stayed with Mrs. Berry after the funeral. Sarah and Anna McCassen told how the gang had passed their house, singing and parading back and forth with Bill Berry in the lead. And last, Edward Pratt told that he gave Henry the warrant to arrest Ike Berry and Britton on charges of inciting a felony. For the People, the evidence closed and the defense offered no testimony."

Anna had liked the story. She had been fascinated by it, was totally absorbed in it; but at the same time, she was disturbed. Such awful men! So many bad things had happened.

"Anna, Anna, do not look so forlorn. It is all over. The men were all caught and put in jail," Poppa assured her. "No one will ever be bothered by them again. This was a long time ago."

The sleepy child relaxed, hugged her parents and siblings, and padded off to bed.

Poppa leaned back in his chair and thought back. It had been a couple of years ago, there had been a piece in the paper. All the parties involved in the Circleville fiasco had served their prison terms and were free men—except Ike, who had been sentenced to life in prison. But after eighteen years Governor Oglesby had pardoned him because Ike was nearing his end with consumption and had only a short time to live. The article had ended with the statement, "The days of Ike Berry are said to be numbered and he will go to the great beyond, where he sent poor Henry Pratt nearly a score of years ago."

And Momma said, "Come, it's late. We must get some sleep."

30

Anna heard the car drive into the farmyard driveway. She was canning grape juice and was pouring the warm purple mixture into jars. The grape harvest of 1946 had been plentiful. The kitchen had a sweet, tart aroma, and Anna's mouth watered in anticipation of tasting the first glassful after it was sealed and cooled. Company was rare on the farm on a weekday afternoon. Grabbing a dishtowel, Anna pulled back the calico curtain and peeked out. It was Emma! Alone. She was coming to the back door with a stricken look on her face. 'Something's wrong,' thought Anna. Holding the screen door open, Anna flatly demanded "What is it?"

Emma looked distraught. "We had something awful happen last night." Pausing, she added, "Everyone is OK."

Anna sighed with relief. Sinking into a kitchen chair, Emma continued.

"Bill and the kids and I were just finishing supper when we heard a loud 'thump' sound outside. Bill went out to investigate and he came back into the house looking pale as a ghost. You know Chief? Our beautiful pony?"

Anna nodded.

Emma continued haltingly. "Well, apparently he was running around the orchard as he's done a thousand times, but somehow he ran into a peach tree trunk and broke his leg."

Anna sat down at the table. She clutched at the buttons on her dress. She had liked that little pony. It was white with black markings that looked like a saddle on both his sides. So unusual.

"Mom, he hit it so hard the bark is knocked off the tree. After Bill told me what happened the kids just wailed. I guess they knew what would have to be done. Bill and I went into the other room. He told me he just couldn't shoot that beautiful little animal, so I said, 'Go to the phone. Call a neighbor until you find someone who will.' And you know what? No one would come. I guess they just couldn't do it either. So I called sister Frieda and they came over. Bill got the gun and I tell you Mom, I never felt so sorry for anyone."

"When he went out the back door I turned the radio on loud and tried to console the kids. But even over the radio I heard the crack of the gun, and my heart just broke. Pretty soon Bill came in and tears were streaming down his face. I followed him as he went to put the gun away. I was afraid to, but I had to ask how it went. 'It went well,' was all he could say. So, we didn't have a very pleasant night at our house."

"I'm so sorry," Anna sympathized. She arose and returned with a plate of peanut butter cookies. Emma recognized the plate. How many times during her childhood had she seen her mother serve delicious morsels from this white plate with the gold etching around the edge. She and her siblings would empty it with small greedy hands almost before Anna could place it on the table. Now the plate had fine lines cracked into it and a tiny chip on one side. Emma remembered how she had, on a night so long ago, bumped the dish on the dishpan when she and Frieda were doing supper dishes. She had been afraid to tell her mother. Needless to say Anna was quite unhappy, but Emma remembered she was not punished.

Now Emma and Anna sat at the table, quietly. Suddenly Emma could see Elly, Albert, George, Frieda, and her parents surrounding her. There was teasing and there was laughter; warmth and good smells. She was a child again, and she reveled in it. But the reverie was broken as Fred came through the back door.

His presence gladdened Emma. She truly loved her father. She yearned to run to him and hug him and feel his big arms around her. But that would not happen. There had never been much hugging and outward affection in the family, and Emma had missed it. But there was love. Much love.

"Emma, what brings you here?"

So Emma repeated the story to him. Fred simply shook his head as she had known he would.

"That's a shame. Poor Bill. It must have been hard on him." Fred sat down at the table and reached for a cookie. He placed it in front of him but Emma noticed he never took a bite. After the three visited for a while, Emma said the kids would soon be home from school, that she had better go, but she didn't want to. She wanted to stay here awhile longer, to be alone with her parents, to feel taken care of and protected, worry free as when she was a child. But no, she must leave. There had never been a time when Emma was not there when her children arrived home.

Fred and Anna walked to the car with Emma. They passed by the old cement horse tank that Fred still kept filled. Emma stopped and gazed into the water, and there were the gold fish swimming lazily. There had been gold fish in the

tank for as long as Emma could remember—deep orange,
beautiful, long fish that had delighted her and her siblings.
She dipped her fingers into the cool water and watched as the
ripples sent the fish scurrying.

A long time ago, a neighbor boy had a hoop that he
pushed with a stick. It was a toy to be envied. Emma had
wanted one. She wanted it so badly that one morning when
she rode with her Poppa to the neighbor's home, she asked
the boy if she could have the hoop. This was a bold feat for
the shy Emma. He said yes, she could have the hoop and
stick, if she would do a chore that his father had assigned him
that very morning. He was to pump the horse trough full,
using the hand pump—no small task. Without a moment's
hesitation, she had agreed. Running to Poppa, she explained
that she would like to stay and visit, and would walk home
later. After Poppa agreed, Emma ran to the pump, and her
small arms wildly pumped the handle as water poured forth.
When she felt her arms would surely fall off, she stopped to
see how much water was in the tank. It must be almost full!
To her dismay, there were only a few inches of water inside.

"There must be a leak in the tank," she exclaimed to the
boy. The amused lad assured her there was none, and he
went to sit in the shade of a nearby tree to observe the tired
and discouraged Emma.

But there was the hoop leaning against the fence,
gleaming in the sunshine. Again, she grasped the red handle
and closed her eyes, imagining herself running down the
road towards home. Only this time, her hands were grasping
a stick and guiding the coveted hoop over the bumps and
gravel until she reached her driveway. Gleefully she would
cross the barnyard and roll the hoop to the back door to
surprise Momma. So Emma pumped. Every so often she
would stop to see how much had filled.

It can't be. I'll never get done!

Finally Emma asked if she could come finish tomorrow. She was so tired.

"No," the boy had answered stubbornly. "Finish today or no hoop."

Emma was not a quitter by any means, so now, as she remembered, she did finish the job. The hoop was hers! But when it was handed over to her there was no running home. Instead, there was a weary little girl trudging along, carrying a well earned treasure in small blistered hands.

Anna and Fred stood and watched their daughter reflect on a long ago memory until she turned and told them goodbye. They watched and waved until the car was out of sight. A cloud of dry, heavy dust was left hanging over the road on that quiet autumn afternoon. Returning to the house, Fred murmured, "Poor old Chief. I really liked that pony."

31

Anna was cutting rhubarb. A sharp knife whacked the stems at the bottom and the big leaves were cut and stacked in a pile. She would place them between the rows of vegetables in the garden to keep away weeds and retain moisture. Sometimes her little girls would take the largest leaves and put them on their dolls for bonnets, but they were all in school now. The school year was quickly winding down. The year had passed so rapidly, but she was glad. The children were needed at home for the tremendous workload that came with the season. Tonight, though, there would be pies for supper—the first fruits of her garden.

Ordinarily, Anna would carry the dishpan of rhubarb into her kitchen and strip away the pink skin. But today the weather was perfect, so she sat down on an upside down bucket and proceeded to peel the stalks. The peels formed a curly mound at her feet. Using her apron, Anna wiped her face. It was then she saw the thing in the sky. *What? What is that?* Rising to her feet and shielding her eyes, she noticed it seemed to be moving closer, hovering in the sky. Anna's heart raced. Picking up her pan, she ran to the front porch. Still it came, slowly.

Fred was in town. *Oh, why can't he be here?* Her gaze became transfixed. As it came closer into view, she saw colors. Wonderful colors. Reds and yellows and greens. It was a balloon! A big beautiful balloon! Anna had never seen the likes. It moved slowly. Closer and closer it came. To this day, Anna didn't know how long she watched, but then the balloon was right overhead, very low. Oh, how she wanted to run out and wave, but she didn't venture far from the porch.

There was a long rope hanging from the bottom of the balloon, and when it passed over, it was so low that the rope fell into the grape vines and dragged the entire length of the vineyard. Pulling slowly upward, Anna watched as her visitor left as it had come. She hoped that the school children had been outside to see the sight.

In the afternoon, Anna stood at the driveway waiting for her children to come into view. *Here they come.* Excitedly, Anna started to meet them. It was probably, she thought, the first time she had ever done that.

"Momma! Is something wrong?"

"No," she had assured them. "Did you see it? Did you see the balloon?"

The blank looks on their faces said 'no'. Oh, how disappointing! Anna had wanted to share the experience, to have them see what she had seen. But no, and neither had Fred.

So, she proceeded to tell her story, to bring it alive and relate the experience she had felt. Fred and the children were thrilled by what they heard, but disappointed also to have missed such a spectacle.

Even today, when she closed her eyes, a beautiful balloon came into view, the same balloon Anna had watched alone that lovely long ago spring day.

32

The medicine man had once again visited Anna's home. He had arrived once or twice a year, trotting his bay into the barnyard, pulling the four-wheeled buggy. Inside the buggy were suitcases of bottles and boxes, all kinds of bottles and boxes filled with liquids and pills that promised to cure whatever ailed them. Anna did not really like the medicine man. He had always watered his horse at the tank without asking, and this displeased Fred. Then the medicine man would haul out and open his many cases, all the while making wild claims of miracles and cures he had witnessed, crediting his vast array of wares.

Anna didn't want to buy his products. She felt uneasy giving her children tonics or other medicines from this traveling salesman. Every morning she had given the children, except for Elly, a big spoonful of Tanlac, a tonic from the drug store. "Elly's too young. She doesn't need it," Anna had explained to the others when they were lined up and the vile tasting liquid was dispensed. "It's good for your blood."

Had she given little Elly the tonic, would Elly have been spared the sickness that later took her life? The question had prodded her mind many times, but she had always pushed the thought aside, and tried not to think about it. The doctor had assured her it was not something she had done, or not done. But doubts would come in the middle of the night, and Anna would toss and turn, wanting to forget, to be rid of any guilt feelings, and also to forget the medicine man.

For one day when he was leaving, and Anna had not made a purchase, he pointed a finger at little Elly and declared, "That one will never live to be old!"

Anna was stunned. She picked up the child and held her tightly. Little Elly, too young to understand, happily waved goodbye as the horse and buggy was lost in a trail of dust as it rattled down the country road. It had upset the two older girls. Questions and tears prevailed. When Anna told Fred, he scoffed. "What does he know? He's just trying to scare you into buying."

Oddly enough, that was the last time the medicine man came around. Anna was relieved. She never wanted to see him again. *But had he been right? Did he have a medicine or herb Elly needed? Or was he some sort of seer, someone with supernatural powers that could look beyond the present? Or just, as she suspected, a salesman, making a living, although a heartless creature at that — one who frightened her and her children. Yet, he seemed so convincing, so sure of himself. And of course, his prediction had come true.*

So the memories of the medicine man were joyless and displeasing, ones she kept to herself and never shared with anyone.

33

It was an exciting time at Anna's home. There was to be a party—a surprise party at that. It was September, 1920. The pastor of the church, Reverend Krietemeyer, would be celebrating the twenty fifth anniversary of his ordination and installation. Because he had served the congregation for a quarter of a century, the members of St. John's decided to celebrate the event in a fitting manner.

The ladies of the congregation, along with the church council, decided upon a surprise in the form of a church service on Wednesday at three o' clock, with a banquet in the evening. The Reverend Witte, of Pekin, who had installed Reverend Krietemeyer so long ago, agreed to preach the German sermon; and Reverend J.G.Kuppler, of Jacksonville, would give the English address.

The plans were laid. On the day set, the pastor would be beguiled to visit Pekin on business. Shortly after, a telephone call would summon him to return home in haste. Fred was a member of the church council. There was so much preparation: contacting fellow ministers, officials of the Lutheran conference; so many letters for the council members to write, anxiously waiting for the replies; so many meetings to compare notes. There would be a collection taken to present to the pastor in appreciation of his services, and it all had to be done secretly!

Then there was the meal. Members were notified to bring food, and lots of it. The church basement had to be readied for the supper without the pastor's knowledge. Could they do it? It was such a tremendous task! Plans were started weeks before, and they seemed to go smoothly, due in large measure to the ingenuity of the pastor's wife. Now it was only two days before.

Anna had washed, ironed, and readied her family's Sunday best clothes. She had baked three pies—two cherry and one blackberry—and tomorrow would kill and dress three chickens that would be fried on Wednesday morning. Her homemade apple sauce would also be removed from the cellar shelves, along with whatever else looked appealing.

Wednesday morning dawned rainy and dreary. Anna arose extra early to start cooking for the afternoon meal. She had hoped for sunshine and good roads, especially for those traveling so far. She was excited, yet uneasy. So much work had been put into this. So much could go wrong. Most importantly was that the speakers arrive safely, and for the inclement weather to not keep people home. Especially important to Anna was the desire to surprise the pastor. The little girl within her still stirred with excitement at the prospect of catching him unaware, but she remained impassive, lest her family suspect.

The children balked at being roused at such an early hour, but when they remembered what was taking place that day, the house, so quiet a few moments earlier, seemed to fairly throb with commotion. Anna could not remember chores being done so quickly and so willingly. Without her asking, the girls prepared breakfast and had it waiting for

Fred and the boys on their return from choring.

The morning quickly passed. Everything was done
except braiding the girls' hair. This was no small task. Three
squirming youngsters were made to sit quietly, for they knew
the more they wriggled, the tighter the braid. Everyone
passed inspection, the food was loaded, and they were off!
The rain still fell, and the roads were soupy, but nothing
could dampen the fervor of the children. Now that Anna was
seated and on the way, she was aware that her stomach was
slightly churning, and she could see that Fred's jaw was
tightly set.

*No, I'll have fun. I'll enjoy this. It will come off well, and will
be a day to remember.*

She had been right. From the account that later appeared
in the newspaper, in spite of the weather, members of the
congregation and visitors from surrounding towns turned
out in large numbers. The pastor had left for his alleged
business appointment. As planned, he had been summoned
by his wife to return home. When he rounded the corner on
the hard road, in sight of his church, he saw the whole place
lined with automobiles and buggies.

Arriving at the church, Reverend Krietemeyer was
received by the church council and invited up the aisle of the
crowded church to a seat of honor in front of the altar, the
council occupying seats to the right and left. The
congregation sang a German hymn before Reverend Witte
preached the anniversary sermon, emphasizing the reason
both pastor and people had to thank the Lord on this
occasion.

An English hymn was sung next and Reverend Kuppler
made the English address. At the conclusion of the address,
Fred's brother, John, in the name of the church council and
the congregation, presented the pastor with a gift in the form

of a check for $300 in appreciation of his services, and by reason of the high regard in which he was held. Anna remembered how Reverend Krietemeyer had responded, feelingly, and heartily thanked the congregation for this evidence of loyalty and love. Other ministers and visitors spoke and extended hearty congratulations on behalf of their congregations. Youngsters were becoming quite restless by the time the service was concluded with the singing of *Now Thank We All Our God.*

In the meantime, the ladies of the church were preparing a sumptuous banquet in the basement. There was no end to the good things to eat. Two long tables were filled six times, and over three hundred people enjoyed the repast—many more than were expected. Humorous toasts, after dinner speeches, and anecdotes were given by the visiting pastors. A good social time was enjoyed for the rest of the evening, and with many hearty good wishes to Reverend Krietemeyer and his wife, the people departed for their homes.

So it was over. The surprise and celebration had been a complete success. Fred and Anna both felt a sense of relief, and yet, she knew a tremendous letdown would hover over her household tomorrow. For weeks their conversations had centered around the surprise celebration. The planning and all the excitement seemed to bring an element of joy and giddiness. Of course there had been other church celebrations, community box socials, and the like, but none had quite compared to this. Anna knew that, with the morrow, all would once again settle into the familiar routine that they were so accustomed to, but the memories would be there for many years. Supper time would be filled with chatter and discussion from each member of the family. With so many at the church, it had been impossible to talk with everyone, so it was wonderful to hear each person share their dialogues and update the family on neighbors, relatives, and fellow churchgoers from so far away.

Never had the church been so full, and would not be again until the passing of their beloved Pastor in December, 1934. Clergymen from many parishes in central Illinois were among the throng that attended his memorial service. Fred had been a pallbearer. Reverend Krietemeyer had been admired by the people of the community, as well as members of his church, and the outpouring was evidence of the esteem in which he was held. For nearly forty years he had served his people, and had indeed served them well. He had been missed, but as always, the Lord provides. It took the congregation a while to adjust to a new person in the pulpit, but the young man and his family that came to fill the vacancy were soon accepted, and would also serve the people well.

34

Anna was sitting under the sprawling branches of the huge hackberry tree that grew in Emma's front yard. It was summer and hot in town, so she was pleased to spend this day in the country. This tree. She knew there was a history to it. It seemed everyone around the rural area where Emma and her family lived was familiar with the 'big hackberry.'

Now she watched her grandchildren and the neighbor children circling the tree on the roots high above the ground, trying to keep their balance. The last to slip off won the game. It was a simple, yet entertaining, way for a child to pass a long summer afternoon.

A rope swing hung from the heavy branch that jutted towards the house. The children were taking turns pushing and swinging, and occasionally twisting the rope tightly and then spinning round till the rider would jump from the seat and slump dizzily to the ground. Their joy amused Anna. She laughed with them, but a deep frustration set in. *I want to do that. I want to swing and twirl and feel the rush of wind in my face. I can remember just how it felt.* She sat quietly, though, with folded hands, and waved to the children when one would shout, "Grandma, watch this!"

There was one side of the large trunk that had been filled with materials to stop the decay that happened many years ago. It was said that the space was so large a man stood inside the trunk and did the necessary repairs to save it. And the tree thrived.

Anna remembered another story, the one that fascinated her the most. It seemed unbelievable to some, but the legend had been handed down and made perfect sense to her.

Emma's home was just a few miles from Circleville, the little town that Poppa had told her about so long ago. Of course, it was long gone, the homes and stores deserted, time and the elements taking their toll until only one building was still standing. It seems that a young Abe Lincoln was the circuit rider that came up from Springfield on his way to the Pekin courts. As a circuit rider, Mr. Lincoln would, for several months each year, travel the judicial circuit, following the judge from county seat to county seat. This way, he could take cases as they came his way.

The Circleville hotel was a convenient stopping off place, and he had stayed there several times. After leaving the hotel, heading toward Pekin, the legend said that Mr. Lincoln would always stop and rest under this Hackberry tree, Emma's tree. It was his oasis. Even today, high on the trunk, a chain with a ring was embedded deep in the bark, put there long ago by someone. She wondered who. This was the chain and ring to which Mr. Lincoln tied his horse as he rested his lanky body under the spreading branches. When the brooding young man felt cooled and serene, he would untie his mount and slowly ride down the road to his next court appearance.

It was quiet in the yard now, she was alone. Anna

imagined the young lawyer dismounting, petting his horse, and stretching out. She felt a closeness, for she believed. The story had been around always, told emphatically and explicitly the same. It was handed down by folks who lived in the area and had the knowledge. In her mind she watched the man and his horse round the curve in the gravel road and disappear.

Anna felt akin to the tree. Both were very old, although the hackberry much more so. She wondered how old. Both were rooted deeply, stationary and stable. Both had spread their protective arms for many years, sheltering, giving refuge and security. But she knew the day would come when both would bow to time, leaving only legends and memories.

35

Anna's young sons were sitting at Fred's feet, enthralled. They never tired of hearing about the time their Poppa went to see Buffalo Bill and his Wild West Show. Newspapers and posters had proclaimed the coming event. Never in a million years had the young Fred dreamed he'd get to attend. For some time, even in this remote farm area, folks had heard about the young man named William Cody. He had killed many buffalo to feed the Union Pacific construction crew in Kansas, hence his nickname. Cody had made a name for himself as a rider for the pony express, an Indian scout, and had been cited for bravery on several occasions. So here was a frontier hero, someone who caught the imagination of many young farm lads like Fred.

News of the wild west had drifted back to the Midwest during the late 1800s, leaving those at home anxious and curious to hear more about what went on in the new frontier. It was not so long ago that Fred's own Poppa had come to this country and been considered a pioneer, helping tame this vast territory. Now another part of the country called to many, and the tales that reached the ears of a youth on the Illinois prairie were spellbinding. Soon Buffalo Bill and his sensational show would be coming!

Anna never did hear Fred say how he traveled the

distance to the show, but she could almost recite word for word the account that Fred would relive.

"When we first arrived at the show grounds, we had some time to look around. Somehow we found ourselves staring at a truly awesome sight—the train that carried the troupes of the show. There were about forty cars. A workman was close by and I asked about the train. He said that it carried several hundred workers and entertainers and all the animals, plus buggies, water tanks, stage coaches for the show, and all the riding gear. They were unloading as we talked and I was very impressed with the precision of the workers.

Hundreds had come to see the big event, and when everyone was allowed to take their seats, I was so excited I could scarcely breathe. I surely was not prepared for the wonderful spectacle that was to happen. First came the grand review. There was a long parade of folks from other countries. And you cannot believe the Indians! It was the first time anyone here had seen an Indian, and all the while, the band called the Cowboy Band played the Star Spangled Banner. Next were the Rough Riders of the World. These men were riders and ropers, and really put on a show. There were dozens of them. They rode horses in such circles and patterns that it almost made me dizzy.

Then the real show began. Buffalo Bill Cody made his grand entrance into the arena. He rode in on his horse... seems the horse's name was Duke. Colonel Cody was very tall. Usually, I don't think one so tall looks good on a horse, but he surely did. I'll never forget his high boots.

Colonel Cody made a short speech and then introduced Miss Annie Oakley. She entered the arena bowing and throwing kisses. Annie was a small girl and wore a short skirt and leggings. About the best shot I ever saw. The first few times she fired, some women and small children were frightened, but pretty soon they were so taken with her that they were clapping right along with the rest of us.

It's a good thing, 'cause for the rest of the show, the shooting never seemed to stop. A man threw glass balls into the air. From no matter what position, Annie never missed the target. Another trick was her famous mirror shot. Annie held her rifle backward over her shoulder and held a mirror in her other hand to see the target. Again and again, she shot and never missed. Then she shot clay pigeons, one after another. And she could even stand twenty feet from the gun, run, pick it up, and fire after the trap was sprung. The crowd loved her.

Then came a reenactment of the Battle of Little Big Horn. So many horses and so much shooting!

Next came dozens of buffalo with Indians and Cowboys chasing after them. What a treat to finally see a real live buffalo.

Oh, and another exciting act was the attack on a stagecoach carrying the mail. Someone said that some of the prominent local townsfolk had been asked to ride in the coach ahead of time...but I didn't know any of them. I found out later that important people were asked to ride the stage in every town. During the attack Buffalo Bill and his Cowboys came to the rescue saving the stagecoach, its passengers and the mail. There was painted scenery for every act, showing mountains, lakes, and such. After every part of the show, the people clapped and cheered.

Finally, with a flurry, the show ended. Buffalo Bill, tall on his horse, rode around the ring, hat in hand, waving goodbye to one and all. I surely hated to see it end. For awhile, I forgot this was just a show. It seemed to really happen. I can honestly say, I've not seen anything like it again."

Finishing his story, Fred sat back and closed his
eyes...remembering. Then his sons ran outside shooting their
pretend guns and riding on pretend horses. Anna had heard
the story many times and always enjoyed it. But deep inside
she was resentful because she wanted to see Buffalo Bill, too.

36

It had been a miserable summer. Army worms had invaded the farm and all surrounding areas. The ugly black creatures with green stripes were ruining crops at an alarming pace. The damage was widespread. Farmers had enough on their minds. A great war raged across the ocean. This was the first war Anna could remember. Someone had named it World War I. *The whole world at war? It didn't seem possible. How was Poppa's beloved village faring? Were her and Fred's unknown kin safe and unaware? Or were they homeless and suffering?* She didn't know.

Then one morning news came that Fred's nephew, who lived close by, would be leaving to serve his country in this senseless battle. Sending young men across a vast ocean to fight on foreign lands angered Anna. Their parents labored and overcame great obstacles to rear a child into adulthood. Sending them away to face being wounded or worse, made all their efforts seem futile. But no matter, next Saturday the family would make the trip to Green Valley and see Harry off.

In the meantime, Fred had decided on a recourse to his own battle. There was a fairly simple, yet laborious, method to rid his fields of the pests destroying his crops. Ditches the length of the field would have to be dug. As the army worms crossed the field, they would fall in and be trapped, unable to crawl out. It seemed strange, but it had worked for others. The boys were young and could help a little, but Fred knew most of the digging would be done by himself.

Early in the morning before the heat set in, Anna watched as Fred trudged to the field, shovel and water bottle in hand, to start his task. All day and into the next, stopping only for dinner, he dug, until at the end of the week he proclaimed the job finished. He had won. As others had told him, it worked. No, it had not completely rid the fields of the plague, but most of the army worms were destroyed, so that once again the crops were able to root and thrive.

Early on Saturday, Anna and Fred gathered their youngsters to make the short trip to Green Valley. The children were excited, but their parents' hearts were heavy.

Nearing the village, they were taken aback by the throng of people. Somber adults, faces drawn, were surrounded by children, laughing and gay. There was a special train that had already arrived to take the young men to their destination.

"We must find sister Anna," Fred said as the crowd pressed around them. "We must tell our nephew goodbye."

Anna almost hoped they wouldn't find them. A lump was already in her throat, for she was watching parents and siblings surrounding their loved ones who soon would embark on a journey, the likes of which they had never experienced. Some would return, many not.

The huge steam engine blasted a whistle signaling the men to make ready. Just then Fred cried, "There they are!"

Elbowing through the crowd, they reached Harry and his

family. Anna couldn't talk. She could look at her in-laws' faces and feel their pain. And when Fred shook his nephew's hand and told him goodbye, tears fell down her face.

Then they were off. The great engine chugged and puffs of smoke and sprays of steam poured out. A sea of waving hands filled the air, and excited children stood on tip toe to see, while others perched on their father's shoulders. Everyone watched as the train slowly pulled away, heading south. There had been no bands, no speeches, no fanfare. The only sounds were muffled sobs, and the clacking of the wheels on the silvery tracks. People turned away, ready to go home. The mood was bleak. Anna said to her sister-in-law, "Come to our house. I'll fix something to eat. You can rest." But she had politely refused. She had explained that she wanted to "get it over with." Facing the house and farm without Harry for the first time would be hard. Best to do it now.

That night many prayers were sent up for the young man's safety, not just from family, but from the whole church community. A long time later, he did return home. Many who served with him did not. So this time, when the train pulled into the station, the tears were of joy. Their nephew was home, safe and whole. Anna and Fred gave thanks.

37

1924. 1924. Why did that particular year linger in Anna's mind? It flashed like a neon sign she had once seen downtown that said EAT. Off and on. Off and on. It tickled Anna. The sign seemed more like a command than an invitation.

Oh, there it was. Yes, December 17, 1924. The winter of the great freeze.

A slight drizzle had started falling from a dark afternoon sky, and as the rain fell, so did the temperature. There had been ice storms before, but not like this one. Heavy rains fell ahead of an extreme cold spell, and then the rain turned to sleet. The full blast hit on December 18. It had affected all the middle states. The kitchen windows were so thick with ice one could not see out. Fred sprinkled ashes and sawdust to make a path to the barn. His animals had to be cared for. The sleet continued throughout the night. On December 19, the thermometer showed two degrees below zero at six AM. Trees creaked ominously under their burden.

The telephone lines sank lower and lower, and one of the girls commented, "It looks like the poles are holding great jumping ropes." Then the spindly poles, encrusted with ice, snapped like twigs. Telephone, telegraph, and power lines were down by the hundreds. The ice also took its toll on the trees. At first small branches and twigs littered the ground, but later the thump of huge limbs pounded the earth until the yard looked like some graveyard for broken and tossed timber. Fred lamented that most of his trees, some standing since before anyone could remember, were now reduced to scraggly trunks. They later learned that the storm was widespread. In Pekin, hundreds of trees fell and blocked streets. Later the newspapers would state that in their own little village of Green Valley the damage had been unusually heavy.

On December 20, the entire area was paralyzed. Again Fred checked his thermometer: eight below zero at six AM. Huge icicles hung from the roof, and the house looked sad and droopy and heavy. He winced as he saw his cherry trees lying in the distance, and he knew full well that none of the other fruit trees had been spared. Gingerly carrying a bucket of water from the pump house, he entered the kitchen where Anna was waiting to make coffee. She let the children, now in their teens, sleep as late as they wanted. There was nothing to get up for. Everything had come to a standstill: no mail, no school, no paper, no phone service. Small villages were completely isolated, and Illinois was a tangle of broken wires. Surrounding states also had feeble communication with the rest of the country.

For days and days they battled the ice. Many people died. Many bones were broken. Trains could not run, and when at last they could, they ran late. The sleet had stopped, but the cold continued and got worse. On December 29, the thermometer had read a staggering thirty below zero. Fred couldn't believe his eyes. In fact, he removed his steamy glasses twice to clean them, but it was so. This was a first, a record, he was sure. By now there had been twelve days of

JOYCE THOMPSON

ice. It had seemed like a hundred. Even though the rain had stopped, the temperature stayed low, so as not to let the ice melt.

Much of the corn was still in the fields. Shucking never started until late fall. Fred knew the stalks would be down and would have to be picked up from the ground. And laundry day had taken a definite toll on Anna. Just getting the laundry to the pump house where her gas powered washing machine stood was no small task, but they coped— they had no choice.

One day, when the temperature allowed, the girls took a sled out to the icy road. The traffic free conditions allowed them to push one another for long distances. Anna had wrapped their faces securely so they would not breathe the frigid air. After a time, the running and sliding had made the girls warm, and the damp frosty mufflers were becoming uncomfortable. While Emma removed the mufflers from her sisters' faces, Frieda noticed a great billow of black smoke in the distance.

"Look!" she called to Emma and Elly. The three girls stood looking for a time before running to the house to tell their Momma. Anna gingerly found her way to the road and saw the ominous sight.

"Fred, Fred!" she cried. "Come quickly!"

It was hard to tell, but they were almost positive where the fire was located. Fred left at once, and was gone for hours. When he did arrive home, the news was somber. Their good neighbors a few farms away had lost their home, a beautiful place, a landmark. It was thought that the fire had started in the kitchen, and with the frozen conditions and all, saving it was impossible. Even worse was the fact that the home had just been remodeled and was filled with many lovely things. Anna remembered, though, that family and

160

neighbors had rallied, the home was rebuilt, and still stood today.

The ice stayed all winter, not giving a hint of leaving until March. But when that first glorious day dawned, the wheels were set into motion. There was corn to pick, damaged wheat to survey, and hundreds of poles to replace. The team of horses would be hitched to pull the trees and branches from the yard, and when it dried, hundreds of twigs would have to be collected by the children and thrown onto a large pile. Finally, when the weather and wind were right, Fred would light the match and all would gather around to watch the fire.

It had been a difficult spring. As predicted, the corn was down and twice as hard to pick. What should have been finished in December, had to be done at planting time. The crops were put in unseasonably late. It had also been an exhilarating time, because not only families, but entire neighborhoods and communities joined together and worked shoulder to shoulder to defeat the devastation that had besieged them. The earth dried, the crops were planted, and the sun shone once again. They had overcome. Gradually the great ice storm of 1924 faded into a misty memory.

38

It had been exceptionally hot and dry during June, 1912. Thinking back, Anna could still feel the heat pouring from her cook stove as she prepared the noon meal that day. She felt out of sorts. Four-year-old Emma had been awake most of the night with an ear ache. Even now the child dozed fitfully on a makeshift bed in the next room. Two-year-old Frieda tugged at her mother's skirt for attention, for she was irritable from the heat. Earlier the boys had been chased outside for being too noisy and disturbing their sleeping sister. Glancing out the window, Anna was satisfied to see them making mud pies by the horse tank. *They'll be a mess, but at least they're out of my hair for a while.*

The newspaper was delivered weekly to the farm, and Fred was almost always standing by the road side anxiously awaiting its arrival. This Friday, with his chair propped back against the wall, he was reading bits of news to Anna.

"Several years ago T.E.Randle loaned an old war relic, a musket with bayonet, to the committee on old relics for the County Fair. It was never returned. Does anyone know its where-a-bouts?"

"Well I sure haven't seen it," Anna grumbled.

Fred chuckled. "Anna, it says here that Mrs. Clements is still quite feeble, and Mrs. Crawford from town had to have her sore finger lanced twice. Look here! Dr. Fink is going to have his house raised eighteen inches from the ground and fill up his yard. He wants to get in dry territory. We talked about that the last time he came here." Turning the page, Fred shook his head. "Here's some more about that big ship that sank a couple months ago. Remember you read that whole story about the Titanic? There are a lot more names and information listed. We should cut this out and save it."

Anna didn't want it. It was all too sad. Things like that are best forgotten. There would be other ships and other tragedies, and in time no one would care anymore.

"Well, well. Stoltz's shoe store is having a sale. Didn't you say just the other day you needed new shoes? It says here 'all styles leather, men's and women's lace or button shoes. $2.85. A $3.30 value.' Maybe we should go in tomorrow and see about getting us both a pair."

Anna never looked up. The potatoes she was frying sizzled angrily, and tiny drops of grease spattered her arms. Gently pushing Frieda away from the heat of the stove and the danger of a spill, she handed her the rag doll Momma had made for Christmas. Both girls had gotten a doll, and the boys got wooden tops. *Children have so much these days. When Fred was a child he had only clothes pins to play with. He had sat for hours, he said, building imaginary things and was quite content.* Anna had offered her sons the clothes pins to build her something and surprise her one day, but they refused. *Spoiled children! Here it is, the 1900s and little ones have no imagination.*

Anna's heart had quickened when Fred mentioned new shoes. She surely needed a pair, for her feet had been aching much. But her sour mood brought the reply, "With the drought, you can be sure the crops won't do well this year. Better to save our money for things we need. And the way the children are growing, I'm sure all four will be ready for shoes in the fall."

"Now Anna," was always Fred's sympathetic reply, for he knew her moods, and knew when to best be still. He silently and longingly read the article from Mr. Firth: "Gasoline engines. A valuable labor saver and money maker. The more you hitch up to an engine, the more money you make and more saving of farm drudgery."

"Come on," Anna was saying. "Call the boys in. Dinner is ready." She pulled the wooden high chair to the table and took Frieda's doll from the child's grip.

"No, you can't have your baby at the table. She'll get spills on her." She set a platter of sausage and the bowl of fried potatoes out. A loaf of bread was placed by Fred's plate along with the bread knife. A big jar of her applesauce was set before them and Anna decided she was too tired to pour it into a bowl.

"Here, just dip it out with this spoon."

Before sitting down, Fred squinted out the window at the bright, hot day. Anna knew he was looking for rain clouds. But there were none.

"Where's your plate?" Fred queried.

"I'm not hungry. Help the baby with her food. I want to see to Emma."

Anna sat down beside the child in the darkened room. She pulled her long skirt above her knees. No one was around to see. How she longed to be free of the cotton stockings and wriggle her toes in the carpet. The long apron she wore only added to the heat, but now lifting it by the hem, it made a wonderful fan to cool Emma and herself. The children seemed to be behaving for their Poppa, for she could hear their quiet chatter. Soon the baby would go down for a nap, and Anna would have to get busy. No plans had yet been made for supper. *Something cool, but what?* She must also tend to her sorry garden. *But now, ahh! The sweet few moments of doing nothing.* It was rare.

Anna closed her eyes. She thought about the things Fred had read to her. There was that feeling again, tugging at her, disturbing her, invading her sense of well being. There had been several social gatherings in town, gatherings made up of ladies belonging to clubs and organizations. There had been teas and dances and committee meetings. Anna had never been to a tea, and had never served on a committee. The thought of it frightened, yet fascinated, her. How she would like to have a very fancy dress. Pink? Yes, a pink, fancy dress like the one she had seen in the Sears catalog; and there was the hat, with a feather arching across the top. She would look nice in pink, going to tea!

Anna imagined tiny tea cakes and silver teapots, lacy napkins, and lovely powdered ladies, looking elegant and refined. And there among them sat Anna, smiling and sipping from a fancy cup, and dabbing her lips with a snowy lace napkin. There was idle chatter and Anna was witty and charming. Then someone was asking her to serve on a committee, and she accepted graciously. Another person called her name.

" Anna, Anna."

"Yes, of course. I'll take more tea." Lifting her eye lids, she stared into Fred's amused face.

"Anna, you fell asleep. Sitting right here in the chair!"

"No. I was just resting my eyes." Anna felt foolish and somewhat disappointed. Yes, she had slept and dreamed—a dream that had reoccurred many times. But it was her private fantasy, a release from the discontent and inadequacy she sometimes felt.

"I have to get back outside. I think the baby is sleepy. The boys can come out with me. Oh, Emma is up and feeling better and I think she's ready to eat."

"That's good," said Anna. "Very good. I'll be right there."

As Fred left the quiet room, she thought, *Does he know? I think so. I'm truly happy here. My home, the farm, the children. I am first and most a farm wife. I wouldn't want it any other way. But I've seen him watching me as he reads the news. I'm always toiling away at some meaningless chore, but does the look in my eyes deceive me? Surely he can see the daily drudgery and how tired I get. But so must he! Still, Fred is so content and everything is a labor of love with him.* Anna felt despair. *I'm so ashamed! I've been so blessed. Why would I want anything more, or to live differently? I get to leave the house on Sundays, and we go to the village on occasion. And weren't we invited to supper only two weeks ago? What's the matter with me? Oh, I'm just feeling sorry for myself. That's what Momma would tell me. And the heat. This terrible heat!*

Pulling herself from the chair, she felt her dress stick to the wooden back. Anna mopped her face with the flowery apron and went into the sweltering kitchen to start her afternoon tasks. And outside, high in a tree, a rain crow cried for rain.

166

39

Pulling herself out of the past, Anna lay her head back and slowly rocked the chair. She felt old. Soon she would be having another birthday. Birthdays...she had seen many. Most had passed without fanfare. Anna couldn't remember many birthdays as a child. However, it seemed the older she got, the more the day was celebrated.

Last month someone had sent Anna a little vase of silk flowers on July 4th. The red, white and blue ribbons caught her eye. Emma came into the room and noticed her mother was smiling.

"What?" asked Emma..

"Our country just had another birthday."

"Yes, it's 1976. America is two hundred years old, Mom."

Two hundred! Well, at least I'm not that old. Fred was born in 1876.

"Just think Emma, our country was only one hundred years old when your father was born. And now another century has passed. We never did much at home on the fourth of July, did we?" Anna pondered.

"No, but few folks your age did. We always have had fire works for our kids. Bill loves the holiday and the fire works. It seems everything he didn't have as a child, he makes up for now. Mom, remember that terribly hot summer in 1936? That was the summer Bill and I took the children out to the country to stay with Frieda and her family. Joyce was newborn, and the heat was causing her problems. Remember what happened on that July 4th?"

Yes, Anna remembered the summer of '36. The heat, and the drought that came with it, smothered Illinois and the rest of the Midwest from mid June into August. For days and days the temperature hit one hundred degrees. Some places recorded one hundred ten to one hundred fifteen. And it didn't cool off at night. Rarely did the nighttime temperature drop below ninety degrees. Paved roads and streets buckled and car tires blew. Many slept on mattresses in their yards trying to keep cool and the city parks were full of weary people trying to get a night's sleep.

Fred and most other farmers worked at night to escape the relentless heat, then helplessly watched their crops wither and die. If the entire crop was not lost, it was stunted and worth very little. Animals suffered, and it was almost impossible to keep the livestock alive. Fred lost a few animals, others lost many. It seemed that four or five hundred people died in Illinois and many more in the rest of the nation. There was not much a person could do but sit under a shade tree. *But we survived. We survived the Great Depression. We were used to suffering and hardships. It seemed almost natural then. I don't think people would do very well today, being so spoiled with their air conditioning. We've grown soft.*

Anna was aware that Emma was talking. She had let her mind wander again. Had Emma noticed? No, she didn't think so. Anna also hoped she hadn't noticed the little jabs of pain that caused her to grimace. She would not have her daughter worry.

" ...so on that hot July 4th we sat in Frieda's front yard and watched our husbands shoot fireworks. Then it happened. One of the rockets flew across the road and landed in the middle of a wheat field. The whole field was full of shocks and the rocket landed smack dab in the middle of one. When the guys saw the fire start to spread they screamed for Frieda and me to start pumping water! Never have two women pumped a pump so fast and so hard. The men each ran across the road with a bucket of water and ran back for another, time and again. The older kids were scared and crying. I don't know how many buckets it took, but finally the fire was out. Just think if the whole field would have burned! But Mr. Weiland was very nice about it, and said it was a good thing that the rocket landed where it did, instead of landing on the loose straw. Now when I think back...my baby was just four weeks old, and Frieda was carrying Dale. We could have both had major problems. But you know how tough the Volk sisters are," Emma laughed.

"I wonder why we weren't there, Emma. I suppose we had our hands full trying to keep things running on the farm. It was just too hot to leave home. Yes, it could have caused problems for each of you. You should have both known better. But I guess you had no choice." The pain jolted through her.

"Mom, are you all right?"

"Yes, yes, I'm just tired of sitting here."

"Why don't you lie down awhile?"

"No. I want to be up. I want to talk. I like remembering."

But Anna was having a hard time talking. It was so much easier to let her mind wander, to muse back in time. *I wish we would have celebrated more on the holidays. Even on our fiftieth wedding anniversary we didn't celebrate. No! Elly had so looked forward to that day. We just couldn't.* She and Fred had simply attended Sunday morning service as they had almost every Sunday throughout their marriage. The small church where Fred had lighted the Christmas tree candles all those years ago had been replaced by a fine brick structure. That morning, after the service, the pastor had invited Fred and Anna to stand by him as the people left the church, and each person warmly congratulated them and wished them many more happy, healthy years. Fifty years...it had gone by in the blink of an eye. They'd hoped to enjoy several more anniversaries together. But then the cancer came, and swiftly reduced her strong, vital husband into a weak, wasted shell. She and Fred were born in Sand Prarie Township and they would be buried there, beside the country church in the grave yard where their parents and all their loved ones rested.

Once again her thoughts returned to her beloved farm. *Did I do right in leaving? Was Fred just trying to make me happy by moving into this house in town? Of course he was. He would have never left. How could I have been so selfish? For the first time I'm admitting to myself I was wrong. Yet, maybe he did find some enjoyment here. He liked the neighbor across the street. And we had much more company since we lived here. We loved sitting on our front porch watching the traffic, and the grandchildren came often. Maybe it wasn't so bad for him. No, it wasn't all bad for him. I was here alone a lot, while Fred went to the farm. I couldn't go back. But it was always on my mind. Every day and every night I thought of my house where I raised my children. My yard, my garden...my life!*

The revelation pounded down on her. It was she who missed the farm, she who wished she'd never left! It took all these years to realize what a mistake she had made. Anna lowered her head. She felt as if a great weight rested on her shoulders. After a time, she removed her glasses and rubbed the back of her neck. *But I can't change things. What's done is done. I'm better off here now. My house will be easy to sell, compared to a farm.*

Anna felt a sense of urgency. Why all the remembering? Why did she feel the need to reveal so many things today; to dredge up old memories, things she had long ago forgotten?

"Emma, sometimes I feel like I've accomplished so little in my life. I've never cured a disease, never made any great discoveries, never even been far from home. I honestly can't think of anything I've contributed to the world. Isn't that why we're here, to leave the world a better place when we die?"

Emma was startled. This didn't sound like her mother speaking. She didn't know she felt that way. But Emma could sympathize, for she too had worked hard and struggled to make a good life for others. She shared her mother's feelings of inadequacies, the feeling that she could have done more with her life.

But how could Mom have these thoughts? She spent so many years sacrificing, raising a family under difficult conditions; working the farm, being strong when most would be weak. Isn't all that the ultimate accomplishment?

Emma took her mother's hand. "Mom, you mustn't feel that way. If anyone has contributed, it's been you. No, you never were in a ladies' club, you never made the society pages of the newspaper, you were never in politics or entertained lavishly. But you were where God wanted you. You were the momma, the wife, and you were always there." Saying this was like a balm to Emma's soul. For she realized she, too, had always been there. *My children, my grandchildren, my beautiful family. That's all I have ever wanted or needed. I would be unhappy doing anything else. Everyone has always said I'm exactly like my dad, but I guess there is a part of my mother in me also.* The two sat quietly, both immersed in thought.

"Emma, can you stay here tonight?"

"Yes, I'll call home. Mom, are you feeling that bad?"

"No, no. I just feel a little punk. And I just want you near me. I wish it was bedtime."

Anna watched as Emma dialed the phone. She relaxed, and a warm feeling came over her. Emma would be here for her. *Tonight I'll sleep and God willing I'll wake in the morning refreshed and without pain.*

But it was not meant to be. As Poppa had often told his family, "For everything there is a season."

Anna had wept and laughed, planted and reaped, mourned and danced, sought and lost, loved and hated, was silent and had spoken.

"A time to be born and a time to die..."

Anna had fought the good fight; her job was done. And that night as Anna lie deep in sleep, God took her into his arms.